M000012777

KINGS AND QUEENS
OF WAR

JULIE KRAMER

Kings and Queens of War © April 2019 by Julie Kramer

Cover by Taurus Colosseum

All rights reserved under the International and Pan-American Copyright Conventions. No part of this book may be reproduced or transmitted in any form or by any means, electronic or mechanical, including photocopying, recording, or by any information storage and retrieval system, without permission in writing from the publisher.

This is a work of fiction. Names, places, characters, and incidents are either the product of the author's imagination or are used fictitiously, and any resemblance to any actual persons, living or dead, organizations, events, or locales is entirely coincidental.

Warning: the unauthorized reproduction or distribution of this copyrighted work is illegal. Criminal copyright infringement, including infringement without monetary gain, is investigated by the FBI and is punishable by up to 5 years in prison and a fine of $250,000.

Blurb

Tara is a War Lady, one of thirteen elite female warriors who protect the War Queen. She is unlike any of the others- unbeknownst to anyone else, Tara has an enchanted tattoo that warns her of danger. She is sent to retrieve the War King of a neighboring country, Luka, and his brother Loxxley. Trials and tribulations hound every step of their journey, right up until the moment that they realize their betrayal will be at the hands of those they trust the most.

Acknowledgments

To my family, for being great support

To Ann, for being the best editor a girl could ask for

To all my author friends and especially Lea (for listening to me gush about all of my covers)

To my readers, for taking a chance on me. Thank you.

Chapter One

As my long fingers fumbled with the heavy silver cloak pin that I was trying to use to hold my cloak in place at my throat, the sharp point stabbed the tip of my index finger. I eyed the ruby drop that welled up from beneath my pale skin and swore vehemently under my breath. Such a mundane task rarely troubled me, but the peals of high pitched laughter from the next room were grating. I half-wished that I could have heard the joke, for surely it must have been amusing to have elicited such an enthusiastic reaction. No doubt the young ladies were giggling about this dress or that gentleman, humdrum, girlish things that irritated me beyond reason. That laughter was the reason that I had accidentally stabbed myself, and I was only glad that I hadn't been holding a knife when my hand had slipped. That would have put an end to this trip before it even began. What a shame that would be.

"Do we absolutely have to go on this particular progress?" I asked. Going on progress was rarely an issue for me either, but the idea of riding across the country for months, surrounded by a gaggle of giggling girls that I was responsible for protecting, nearly sent me out the door in a shrieking panic. Going on progress was an unfortunate necessity for women of our status, a way for us to ensure that the War Queen's subjects weren't becoming restless or planning some sort of uprising. Traveling through the country on horseback, meeting everyone, be they noble or peasant, was entertaining. It was our chance to meet the next generation of warriors, whether they be male or female. However, I had serious doubts about this particular group of young women. They would not be warriors, and I wasn't sure I could keep my temper under wraps for long enough to discern what kind of noble lady they would be when they finished their training at finishing school. It was an amazing opportunity for them, but I would have looked on it more fondly if I didn't have to escort them there safely.

"War Ladies do not *whine*," Lana informed me primly. "Your queen would be very disappointed in your attitude." I bit back the urge to point out that she was Lana's queen as well, which was a true statement but not one that would change Lana's mind or attitude. She was one of the other War Ladies, sprawled across a plush cushion, her long legs crossed neatly at the ankles and her full lips pressed together. Her long blonde hair glittered in the bright light that shone through the windows of our solar, where all of the War Ladies met for important gatherings. The room was an eclectic mix of tastes, weapons shining against the floral wallpaper, a thick rug with a parade of prancing does stretched across the floor. Thick cushions and wingback chairs provided seating. A round table in the corner constantly held food, small treats like pastries or finger sandwiches, and various other refreshments. The floor on the far side was without carpet, a circle carefully marked out on the flat ground; a dueling circle, in case we were ever bored while waiting for a meeting to start. The glistening tile was easy to scrub free of blood if we injured one another; an expensive rug, not so much. I stood in front of the full length mirror, checking my appearance once more before we left.

"No, she wouldn't," I snorted, brushing my long bangs impatiently away from my face so that my violet-gray eyes were visible. "She would laugh at me."

"Indeed she would," Eili chimed in. The ringing laughter of the other War Ladies coincided perfectly with the giggles from the next room. I rolled my eyes slightly at their smug expressions, but let it pass. They knew exactly how such feminine things annoyed me. I suspected that was the reason they did it, and I refused to rise to the challenge.

"Yes, Tara, we absolutely have to go on *this* progress," was the answer from Eili. Her deep brown eyes were patient as she explained, with little thought for the delicate fingers that wove a spiked strap through her ebony hair as she spoke. Almost all of us with longer hair wore a similar strap. Almost all of us *had* longer hair. It was a danger for fighters like us, much easier to grab a handful of, but we were all good enough fighters that we could risk it. Or too vain to be out of fashion. Depending on which of the War Ladies we were referring to, it could have been both. "The King of Mareen has requested a meeting with the War Queen's emissary, you, as soon as possible."

"But why now?" I inquired. "We could be there in two weeks if we rode out now. Three at most."

"The King of Adanesa has asked us to escort the young ladies to their academy," Reaga explained. I already knew that, but she seemed to think that I needed to be reminded. I knew *why* we were escorting the girls; I just didn't know *why* we couldn't do it a little more quickly. "He would take great offense if we backed out of our agreement now. It would be dishonorable. He might even use it as an excuse for war."

I sighed. A part of me was tempted to say let him come, because I was itching for some action, but my duty was to my

Queen first and foremost. If we were lucky, we would have time to spar on the road. We all craved a challenge, so any excuse for a round would be welcome. Honestly, we were probably going to be trying to kill each other most of the time, and only half of that would be in jest. I couldn't remember the last time that a War Lady had seriously injured another, but we had our fair share of cuts and bruises. Most of our bouts began with both of us holding our preferred weapons and ended with us rolling around in the dirt. Not exactly the most dignified approach, but as long as the War Queen wasn't with us, there was no one to disapprove. No one that mattered, at least.

Another chorus of giggles and my hand moved to the hilt of my sword of its own volition. Lana clucked her tongue disapprovingly. "I doubt King Obron of Adanesa would appreciate if you drew your blade on his daughter, either," she chided drolly.

I nodded reluctantly and pressed my sword back into its sheath, although my hand still rested on the cool metal. "You're right," I admitted, as much as I hated to. I shifted, checking my appearance one last time. My weapons were buckled in place, as was my cloak. Tight black leather trousers were tucked into high black boots. Part of the trousers were obscured by a deep indigo dress that was shorter in the front and long in the back, the front resting across my thighs, the back brushing the back of my knees. The stomacher was made of tightly woven silver chain mail. The sweetheart neckline across my breasts led into more chainmail that flowed over my shoulders. My thick, deep brown hair was braided tightly and dangled between my shoulder blades, the locks hiding a spiked strap. It was depressingly common for women in battle to get their hair yanked, but the spikes did a fine job of putting a stop to that foolishness. My violet-gray eyes were clear and shining, the light from the tall, arched windows making my pupils contract to tiny pinpricks. I blinked once, and they returned slowly to normal. I turned to the others; they drew to attention, alerted by my manner that something was about to happen. I glanced out the window and into the courtyard below. The Queen wasn't with us today, which meant that I was in charge. If that meant putting up with the petty squabbles of a pack of irritating young women and my equally loud comrades in arms, then so be it.

"We ride out in an hour."

Chapter Two

The enormous black horse shifted, long mane swishing. Its huge hooves lifted high, nearly to its chest as it pranced; the groom's face was ghostly white as he struggled to contain the beast's enthusiasm, leaning his full weight on the double reins to keep the beast on the ground. His grip on the reins was white knuckled. I took them from him with a grin, smiling as the black horse lowered her head and sniffed me, nostrils flared, the lining pale and webbed with veins. The short black hairs of her muzzle were soft as velvet. The strands of her long forelock covered the bridle down her broad head, a stylized silver lion head surrounded by silver studs and held in place by delicate silver chains in the shape of an X. An identical silver lion was centered on the strap across her deep chest, connected to the polished black saddle. I stroked the length of her long nose gently, then planted my left boot in the stirrup and swung up easily, settling my black cloak behind me across her powerful hindquarters, as well as the short tail of my dress. Their length draped over the top of her wavy black tail, which was so long as to drag on the ground when she shifted. I had been riding for years, riding *Sin* for years. I loved it on a good day, but the prospect of the upcoming miles was enough to dampen my spirits slightly. Not so much because of the distance, which was not the longest I had ever ridden nor would likely be, but more because of the company that I would have to keep. In my opinion, there was nothing better than riding fast through the countryside with no one around, but that wouldn't be happening anytime soon.

As if she sensed my misgivings, Sin turned to look at me, her liquid brown eyes warm as she bumped my knee gently with her muzzle. I patted her arched neck, startled as always by the flare of translucent skin, pearly white, against the ebony of her coat. I was paler than the other War Ladies, despite the fact that I spent just as much time in the sun as they did, and Sin was the darkest of the mounts that we rode. They tended more toward grays or bays, with Sin being the only black and the War Queen's mount the only white. My pale skin, and my clothing, as well as the butt of my pistol, all made for a riot of colors against her dark coat. When I wasn't mounted, I wore the pistol and its accessories on the back of my belt. Even now there was a small pouch hooked on, containing a few thin flutes of black powder and musket balls, as well as a short, thin rod to clean it with. The pistol itself was hooked to the strap of Sin's saddle, within easy reach if I needed it. For long rides such as this, I placed my sword and long daggers next to it. They rattled against Sin's shoulder as she shifted, but they were strapped so that they wouldn't tangle in her long legs or otherwise hinder her motion. The weapons may have been a nuisance, but she was used to them by now. They were strapped to her right shoulder. I could use both hands with some degree of proficiency, but I preferred to use my right hand; it was simply more comfortable for me that way. With them on her right shoulder, I could draw any of the weapons with my dominant hand. Plus, depending on the angle that the enemy was facing, the weapons might be hidden from their view entirely. All of these things I had taken into consideration when choosing the saddle and the straps for the weapons, which were specially made, like most of my equipment.

I grasped the wrist of my fingerless leather gloves and pulled them on, holding the double reins loosely against Sin's neck as we waited, patiently for some but impatiently in my case. Ever one to make her own entertainment, Sin bounced her chin against her chest and I rolled my eyes fondly. We waited in the courtyard of the castle, behind the drawbridge, which was already lowered in preparation for our departure. Sin's iron shod hooves struck sparks on the stones as she stomped, and I allowed her to weave in a slow circle to alleviate some of the tension. Her ears pricked, and I followed where her head was pointing. Tall braziers were being extinguished, the night's coals splashed into darkness by small children, only to be rekindled again that evening. Their faces were pale with ash, the rich colors of the royal livery sullied by smudges of ash and flakes of burnt wood. Guards patrolled the top of the castle, yawning widely, only to snap their jaws shut when the eyes of a War Lady fell upon them. The switch in shifts wasn't for nearly another hour, so they had best be vigilant.

Eili, the most diplomatic of the War Ladies, struggled to corral the young noble ladies. Elegant carriages of all designs waited to be filled, doors with elaborately painted seals held open by carefully impassive drivers. Perfectly polished reins and harnesses jingled softly as the horses shifted, their artificially darkened hooves sparking on the cobbles, shifting the patches of straw that had been laid down to make them more comfortable. As large as the palace was, it was not equipped to handle this many carriages and horses. The ladies had come in at different times, some a few weeks ago, others as recently as the day prior to our trip. The first few carriages had the advantage of shelter for the carriages and stabling for the four horse teams, but those later arrivals had not been afforded the same luxuries. All of the War Ladies had been asked to remove their horses from the stables. For some, that meant renting a stall in one of the liveries in the city, a small enough expense that nevertheless caused its fair share of grumbling. I didn't live in the castle; I was just as happy to take my horse elsewhere, with the added benefit that a bit of room would be opened up for the finer, daintier horses that were our guests.

Full skirts swished as the ladies entered the courtyard, their slippers scuffing on the hard stones. A few of them seemed to be giving Eili difficulty. Sin took one step in anticipation of my command, but Eili held up her hand to forestall me. I stopped Sin as the young ladies climbed, finally, into the carriages, with a great eruption of chittering voices and high pitched giggles that made Sin flatten her ears and toss her head, her iron shod hooves striking sparks as they struck stone. I felt the same. Eili bustled around, nudging the young ladies into their carriages when they weren't fast enough for her tastes, then making an almost frantic motion at the footmen to close the doors. If I didn't know any better, I would have said that she was trying to contain them. I coughed into my fist, hiding my smile as she shot me a dark glare, swinging onto her horse's back.

"You did this," she accused. "Because you didn't want to deal with them."

She meant the fact that she'd had to deal with the girls instead of me, while I got to sit out here in the freezing court-yard on my horse. In my opinion, it was an even trade. I shrugged one shoulder. "Perhaps," I conceded. "But then again, imagine how much longer we would have been here if I had been the one to coax them all out here." Even she had to concede that point with a slow nod. It was supposed to have been my job, but the greatest perk of being in charge, even if it was just for a few days, was that I could delegate my duties. Like, say, make Eili deal with the gaggle of giggles instead of me. Maybe it was selfish. I could live with that.

Eili shot me one last dark look. I urged Sin forward to take our place at the front of the caravan, already chafing at the delay as we rattled across the sturdy wooden drawbridge. Not only were the carriages going to slow us down, we would also be forced to stick to roads so that they could travel; carriages didn't tend to travel well on rugged roads or through rivers, whereas we riders could go anywhere our horses deigned to take us. Without the slow carriages, we could leave the beaten path and ride, although perhaps still not as quickly as I would have liked, I'll admit. There was no speed that could be reached with a large group that would be fast enough for me, which was just another reason that I preferred to ride alone. With them, we were stuck in this long train, a massive moving target for any who chose to attack. The danger made my skin crawl, but my tattoo hadn't alerted me to any actual danger, so we were alright for now. Bored at the sluggish pace, I reflected on history and how we had gotten where we were. They deserved only the best, after all.

Legend goes that a warrior king and queen had fallen madly in love in the midst of a war. When the War was finally over, they had returned home together, overjoyed to discover that the queen was with child. Over the years, more of their children were born. The king and queen raised their children as they ruled their kingdom, fairly and wisely. That all changed when the king and queen were once again called away to war. With no other options, the queen took her daughters, the king his sons, and they went their separate ways for the last time.

When the War was over, the children stayed where they had spent their last years. They had created new governments in honor of their parent's legacy. I lived in Antille, where the warrior queen's daughters had settled. Every year, young women from all over the country swarmed the capital city for a massive tournament. These were challengers for the thirteen open War Lady positions, which the current War Ladies held until they could no longer defeat the challengers or they chose to step down. The highest ranking War Ladies could eventually challenge the War Queen for her title, which was a provision made so that no one who wasn't qualified found themselves ruling a country. We War Ladies were trained in everything that one would need to rule a country, not that all of us wanted to. The same arrangement was set in place for Mareen, only with men.

We War Ladies were many things. Elite warriors, guardians, those who kept the wolf at the door at bay. We served as companions and, occasionally, diplomats, though we were far better warriors than we were speakers. However, we served in whatever capacity our queen asked of us. It was a common opinion that one day I would challenge the War Queen for her throne, but as with most common opinions, it was wrong. I lacked the lust for power that most challengers had. I was not the highest ranking War Lady, but nor was I the lowest; I was content with my place. To me, being a War Lady wasn't about power, or rank, or travel. It was about helping others, and seeing to it that no one ever went through what I had.

A sharp, high-pitched whistle jerked my attention back to my surroundings. My head shot up, instinctively swiveling back toward the War Lady who had whistled. I recognized every War Lady's whistle, and since several of our number were absent, on a hunt with the queen, it was even easier to pinpoint the source of the sound. That was Eili near the back, and I glanced around in an attempt to discern what the warning whistle was referring to.

One of the dainty young women poked her head out of the window of the carriage, brushing the velvet curtains out of the way impatiently with one gloved hand. I urged Sin toward her, cantering past and then wheeling, holding her close to the door so that I could speak with the young woman within. Sin's long forelock swished as she shook her head, fighting my tight hold on the double reins. She was about two seconds from bucking, so I reluctantly loosened my grip.

"What do you think you are doing?" I demanded. "Get back in there. It's not safe." We were going out of our way to escort them, and as such, we were required to provide protection for them. The least they could do was make it easy on us. Then again, when is anything ever easy? Certainly not now, because she ignored me, swiveling her head and searching her surroundings intently. I did as well, worried that she may have heard something that I hadn't, no matter how unlikely that may have seemed. Birds chirped their high-pitched performances high in the trees and a stream rushed nearby, all sounds that a healthy forest would make. Sin's ears flicked, but she was too relaxed to have heard anything out of the ordinary. The swaying leaves of the forest lacked the dead silence that would have indicated the presence of an intruder. When it became clear the girl wouldn't do as she was told and return to the carriage, I waved Eili forward with an irritated sigh. She and her white-blazed bay trotted forward to take my place at the head of the caravan, which was moving so slowly as to still be mostly in sight.

"What?" I growled. Another head popped out, pushing the golden head aside roughly. Curious eyes peeked from behind. The two squeezed in the window, a petite waif with tight golden ringlets and her opposite, a hard faced girl with savage beauty and waves black as ink, studied me critically. The black haired girl sneered down her long, aristocratic nose at me; the blonde leaned forward eagerly. She was crowding Sin, who stepped sideways before I brought her back into place.

"Where are we going?" the blonde questioned eagerly. I considered ordering her back into the carriage and riding on regardless of whether she listened or not, but the knowledge that she probably wouldn't listen gave me pause. If I left her and she was injured with her foolishness, that would be my fault and none other. To leave her in danger because I didn't want to speak to her simply wouldn't do. That was the coward's way out. I had to deal with this myself.

I took a deep, steadying breath. "We are meeting with Ge-," I corrected myself hastily. Ladies of a noble background would be shocked to hear the War Queen, the leader of this country, referred to by her first name rather than her title. We were such good friends that I often forgot that she was my liege, at least until those times that she chose to put me in my place. Those instances were pleasant for neither of us, but whatever my feelings on the subject, it wouldn't do for the noble ladies to return home carrying tales of a queen that couldn't keep her warriors under control. "Her Majesty the War Queen. She and a few of her War Ladies are on a hunt a few miles from here. We will join them at their campsite to rest for a few hours, then continue on and camp for the night further along."

Despite how quickly I had corrected myself when using my liege's Christian name, it was too late. The ebony haired girl had caught the slip. She flipped her mane of hair over one slim shoulder and sniffed disdainfully, cocking one dark brow.

"What did you almost call her?" she sneered. "Her first name?" She shook her head and clucked her tongue, which was just as irritating as when Lana did it. More so, in fact. As she spoke, the girl fingered the solid gold brooch that held her velvet cloak in place at her delicate throat, the center set with an enormous, sparkling emerald. It took me a moment to realize that she was subtly mocking my own functional clothing. The realization brought a grim half-grin to my mouth. Perhaps my outfit wasn't nearly as beautiful as her full dress, but I was not ashamed of my clothing. Unlike her, my clothes were comfortable. My clothes were tight, as they were meant to be to allow motion, but she probably couldn't breathe with the corset strapped around her chest. I lifted my chin proudly and looked her dead in the eyes, even as she said something that made me stiffen, straight as a rod in my saddle. "What kind of monarch allows her subjects to address her by her given name?"

My left hand crept toward the dagger hidden at my back, hooked onto my belt and hidden beneath the cloak pinned across my chest at my left shoulder. "You will not speak of her that way," I ground out between my teeth, my voice deathly silent. Damage had been done to my throat from various accidents, so my voice sounded like pebbles scraping together at the best of times. These were not those times. Finished with the girls, regardless of the fact that they had not done as I ordered, I reluctantly pulled my hand away from my dagger and raised my voice. "Eili!" The caravan had slowed to a rolling halt, but Eili was hidden from my sight, so I was irritated when she didn't answer my summons. "Eili, get back here!"

"She must have gone ahead to scout," Cian observed. Her gray mount pranced impatiently as she pulled up next to me, the smoky mare tossing her head in protest of Cian's tight hold on the reins. "Do you want me to check on her?"

I shook my head sharply, secretly glad to have an excuse to leave the obnoxious girls to their own devices, although a tiny voice reminded me that I was responsible for their safety, even if they didn't deign to respond to my orders. On the other hand, my temper was already shot from the grating giggles, veiled insults, and snail's pace. If I didn't leave soon, these pampered little flowers would see what a War Lady could really do. "I'll go."

I tapped my heels lightly to Sin's flanks; she leapt forward eagerly. Her huge strides ate up the short distance to the front of the caravan in mere moments. I leaned forward in my saddle to search for Eili, but despite my repeated calls, there was no answer. The forest had quieted alarmingly. My heart was in my throat and I had difficulty swallowing, but I pushed forward. Sin pinned her ears and slid to an abrupt halt; at the exact moment, the tattoo on my shoulder seared like I'd been branded. I clapped one hand to it with a pained hiss and grabbed for the reins, but Sin's sudden stop, combined with the blinding pain from my tattoo, dulled my senses. I twisted as I fell out of the saddle to keep myself from going beneath her thrashing hooves. My body jolted as my boots hit the ground.

"This is not the time," I gritted out, doubled over from the pain and fighting to hold my rearing mount, when I saw what had startled her so. An eerie, black fletched arrow jutted from the soft ground between her huge hooves; another was snapped in half on the ground before her, still streaked with blood where it had slashed her shoulder. My ill-timed tumble from Sin's back had prevented that arrow from being in me. Once again, Sin had saved my life.

Still half-blind with pain but spurred by the realization, I straightened with difficulty and drew my sword with a hiss of polished steel. Gathering my strength and turning so that I was back to back with Sin, I searched the forest for signs of the intruder. Only when I glanced back to see how far away the caravan was did it occur to me that I should have warned the other War Ladies of the ambush the moment I realized it.

"Fool," I hissed at myself under my breath, then raised my

voice. "Ambush!" Sin jolted with surprise, or at least I thought it was surprise. Fire and lightning and blistering pain ripped through my tattoo, obliterating any sense but pain. I slid bonelessly to my knees, unable to stop the fall or move, and had just enough time to hope that the warning had been enough to save the others before I tipped forward and saw no more.

Chapter Three

When I finally woke, I knew someone was dead. It wasn't just a feeling, it was a knowing, in my bones as much as in the dull, sad throb of my tattoo. I cracked my eyes open, blinking back the tears that welled from the close proximity of the lantern, the flickering yellow flame waving in the edge of my vision. It was hooded, as it was during the day, kept in readiness when night was about to fall. Everything hurt, but most of the pain was from my shoulder, which felt unusually heavy. I reached for it; a hand came out of nowhere, the long, slender fingers gripping my wrist lightly to keep me from touching the limb.

"Leave it be. You need to rest."

As was true of most things, of course I didn't listen. I pillowed my other hand in the soft, clean material that shrouded my body and pushed myself slowly up to a sitting position, swaying from the pain. A protesting squeak edged from my lips as I realized that even my hand was injured, a large crimson crescent visible through the clean ivory bandage. I could feel the pinch and burn of stitches. There were so many questions that I needed to ask, like what had happened to my shoulder to so damage my magical tattoo, but the first thing out of my mouth was: "Who died?"

Cian's mouth tightened, her rosehip-red lips pursing until they seemed white. She looked down at the floor, even as the other War Ladies stepped forward, crowding around the cot. I performed a silent headcount, running through a mental list to see who was present. Reaga was there, blood smeared across one high cheekbone and tiny flecks of black powder clinging to the tips of her fingers; gunpowder, from firing her pistol who knew how many times. Cian looked even worse, the entire left side of her face scraped and bloody, with a trail of dried blood beneath her nose and the creamy skin about her left eye dark with color that shouldn't have been there. All of the other War Ladies were in various stages of the same disarray, faces dark with blood, black powder, and mud. Clearly none had bothered to clean up; the only wounds that were clean were the ones that had required additional care. The bright white of bandages flashed with subtle movements, which reminded me of my own wound. I touched my fingertips to the bandage gently; the magical tattoo gave a dull, warm throb, almost as if in response. Although the motion was partially because of the reminder that I, too, had been injured, there was another reason. I had realized who was missing from our number; I closed my eyes tightly, my fingers clenching and unclenching in the soft white bed covers so hard that my short nails carved pain into my palms through the thin material.

"Eili." A soft exhalation filled the room, one of combined loss, but none so much as mine. Eili had taken my place at the front of the caravan. If I had returned to it any sooner, or simply not stopped to speak with the ladies, I would be the one being sighed over, my body laid out in a tent to wait to be returned to the tomb of the Ladies of War, a massive marble mausoleum in the capital city second only in size and grandeur to the tomb of the War Queens themselves. Any War Lady that died in battle would be buried in that monument. I felt that one day I would be too, as it was for most a foregone conclusion that I would die in battle, but even in death I would be kept apart from the others by a status no other could claim, at least not in recent memory.

Only once I looked around after the news had sunk in did I realize where I was. The last thing I remembered, we had been a few miles from the castle, halfway between there and where the War Queen's hunting party was camped for the day. They must have moved me while I was insensible, which meant I had been out for at least an hour, probably more to transport a bevy of wounded War Ladies and carriages full of tittering young women who had no doubt been terrified out of their wits after the attack. There was no real way to tell how much time had elapsed while I was dead to the world, and I was afraid to ask.

I bit my lip until it tingled and swung my long legs over the side of the cot, lurching to my feet. A crowd of lithe bodies tensed in preparation for my fall, but I steeled my resolve and remained upright by sheer force of will. The other War Ladies stepped aside as I staggered through them, throwing the mouth of the tent aside and nearly running into the hitching post as my pain-drunken strides pushed me to the side. Sin came up in a half-rear, her huge front hooves knocking into the sturdy wooden bar and the strong leather of the double reins straining to hold her powerful body in place. My uninjured palm resting on the post for balance, I worked with the other to untie the complicated knot that was required to keep any of our mounts in one place, since the intelligent beasts had long ago discovered how to untie the simpler knots. I imagined it wouldn't be long before this knot fell into that number as well, but for right now, with my mind addled with pain and grief, it took me far longer than it should have to release the catch. I leaned against Sin's huge shoulder for support as we walked toward the largest tent in the temporary camp, surrounded by courtiers. Seeing my steely expression, they stepped aside as I reached the mouth, although a general protest did go up when I merely dropped Sin's reins and stepped inside, pushing others out of my way by sheer force. It seemed that I had interrupted an argument, but my news was too urgent to wait. Geneva, the War Queen, argued animatedly with a young man, his once shaggy locks of ebony hair carefully groomed as befit his rank and status. He wore very few weapons, a sturdy rapier, the golden hilt inlaid with a massive sapphire that Geneva claimed matched his eyes, the same eyes that turned to me now, almost pleading, and a short dagger at the small of his back like mine.

"Tell Ellis that it is not his job to tell me what I can and cannot do," Geneva said tightly, The knotted muscles of her upper arms bunched as she crossed them over her chest. Ellis threw his hands up in protest, lips tight and nostrils flared. His blue eyes blazed like the heart of a flame.

"And tell her that it is my job, and she knows I'm going to do it, and if she doesn't like it she should find a new consort," he shot back. I sighed darkly, once again sorry for interrupting a private conversation. I had been there the first time that the two had met, Geneva a young, up and coming War Lady ordered to hunt down Ellis for taking the previous War Queen's scepter. Although he had been innocent of the crime, the last War Queen had refused to acknowledge that; the argument had ended with Geneva challenging her for the throne, and winning. Even then they had loved one another, but their spirits wouldn't allow them to act like they did, so to this day they still fought like cats and dogs, although I didn't know why they bothered. Everyone knew how madly in love they were, which made their massive arguments so entertaining to the rest of us. Unless, of course, you happened to have the misfortune of stumbling into one. Only I was that lucky.

"Before I say anything, might I ask what this particular feud is about?"

Geneva opened her mouth, but Ellis beat her to it. "The War Queen thinks that it is her job to hunt down the killer of her War Lady, despite the fact that she knows how dangerous it is and knows that she has prior engagements that cannot be pushed aside in favor of satisfying her latest vendetta," he finished with a gasp, having said this spiel all in one breath.

"It isn't your job," I said before Geneva had a chance to put her input into the pot. "It's mine." The words were said with bravado, but they felt pathetically ironic considering the shape that I was in at the moment. I straightened, wincing.

Geneva turned to look at me, but she stopped when she noticed where my hand was, laid very gently across the magical tattoo on my left shoulder, still covered with the bandage; I wanted to illustrate my point, but even the lightest of contact made it throb, which was alarming. Very few people knew what she and I did about the mark; even Ellis knew only the basics. She nodded slightly to me, then one hand shot out to grab Ellis' collar, dragging him down from his height enough that she could whisper in his ear. He protested quietly; she repeated the order, motioning to me. Finally he nodded and strode toward the mouth of the tent, touching my uninjured shoulder lightly as he strode by me. I silently thanked any deity that might be listening that he had chosen the shoulder that wasn't injured. It wasn't difficult to tell, because the white of the bandage was visible through the slash in my dress. I would have to change before I did anything else, but Geneva wasn't in the mood to wait.

"So what is this about?" she demanded. When not in the presence of others, excluding Ellis, we addressed one another on equal terms, which sometimes made my mouth or my temper run away with me and get us both into trouble. I took a moment to very carefully phrase what I would say next to prevent this from being one of those occasions.

"I can find them, with this." I motioned to my shoulder, although we both understood that I meant the tattoo, which thumped a steady drum of pain. "But only if you let me go now."

The heavy tail of Geneva's leather dress swished on the opulent rugs as she sat in the chair that served as her throne. She had a throne back at the castle, but any chair that she sat in became a throne due to her proud bearing, which looked more beat down at the moment. One elbow rested on the arm of the chair and she rubbed her head with her fingers, as she always did when she couldn't decide what to do.

"I don't doubt that you can do what you say, but I can't allow you to. You must go to the King of Mareen, as assistance for his guards."

I frowned thunderously, but bit my tongue as she continued. "You will ride alone to his palace, and bring him, in disguise, to speak with me." The situation must truly be desperate if I must ride alone, as she had forbidden it. War Ladies were popular targets, and even the greatest warrior may be felled by an unlucky blow. She had ordered that every War Lady must be accompanied at all times, at least on missions. In my free time, she could not command that of me; I liked my privacy too much. Despite my disappointment about not being able to pursue Eili's killers, I consoled myself with the thought that I could find them after I had finished this important errand for Geneva.

Realization dawned. "So everyone will think that I have been summoned to him, when in fact he is coming to you." Geneva's nod confirmed my train of thought. It was a good plan, but it smacked of a catch. Nothing in my life could possibly be so easy.

"Is there anything else?"

Geneva hesitated, proving my theory that there was more to the story. She bit her lip and toyed with the loose strands of hair that had fallen out of her tight coronet. Her crown was just that, no tiara like other women in power wore to make them seem less than their man. Now that I thought about it, Ellis hadn't been wearing his crown while he'd argued with Geneva; I glanced around, finally noticing it tossed carelessly onto the cot in the corner, no doubt thrown in a fit of rage. The dark iron was a quieter compliment to her shining silver. The sharp spires were studded with sapphires, rubies, and peridots, with one massive diamond in the center of the perfect circle that fell in the middle of her forehead. It looked like a very uncomfortable crown, but she wore it day and night, at least until the occasion of battle arose, when she replaced it with a bejeweled helm, of which she had many.

"Yes," she said finally. She rose from her chair and stepped to the short desk that she always had with her, flipping back the top of a jeweled inkwell and dipping the tip of an eagle feather quill gently into the dark, murky liquid. A piece of chalky parchment was laid carefully out on the table, the corners held down with two heavy glass paperweights shaped like eagles, wings outspread and sharp talons gripping the rocks that they were perched on. The quill scratched as it skipped quickly across the paper, and I felt a pang of sadness. When I had met Geneva, her handwriting had been passable at best, and she'd had no urge to change it. She had grown up in a noble family, the exact opposite of my upbringing, but her unwillingness to participate in anything academic made her reading and writing barely legible. Clearly it was a trait that had to go, as a War Queen must be able to send legible missives, but it made me sad to see such a change forced on her by her station. Her once illegible handwriting was now filled with ladylike swirls and loops, something so unlike her personality that it made me cringe inwardly. I had grown up with very little education whatsoever, so when I had become a War Lady and been given the opportunity to learn to read and write properly, I threw myself into the task with a fervor I had not as yet achieved in anything but fighting and horses. Even so, my handwriting was not like Geneva's, passable but not fancy. I didn't mind the difference. I rarely had the opportunity to write much of anything, so it didn't much matter.

"Tell me," I demanded, finally fed up with her evasions. Her back was hunched over the writing desk. The quill slowed on the paper, until finally she lifted her sharp chin to look at me.

"This assignment is very dangerous," she said finally. I blinked and my brows drew together in subtle confusion. Everything was dangerous; it was the way of the world. We spent every day of our lives training with swords and pistols so that we could fight. Sin could be in a foul mood tomorrow and trample me to death. Another of the War Ladies might get an unlucky swipe and behead me. The fact that Geneva had specifically mentioned that this mission would be dangerous did not bode well for me. "We believe that information about the scheme has been shared. Anyone who embarks on this mission will be in the utmost danger at all times."

I gave her a dry look. "Every mission is dangerous. The sooner I do this for you, the sooner I can find Eili's killers. I'll go." Without waiting to be dismissed, I turned and strode out of the tent, flicking the flap aside with my bandaged hand and snatching Sin's reins with the other. She threw her head up with a protesting whinny, torn away from the lush grass that she had been munching on. She followed me a little too closely in retaliation, her huge hooves all but trodding on my heels as I lead her toward the horsemaster's hastily erected tent. Master Risto was outside, as was his apprentice, Jemmy. It took all of Jemmy's strength to hold a bucking gray gelding in place as they struggled to pull a crossbow shaft out of his shoulder. I recognized Laith's finicky mount and moved to his head, hoping to calm him. I had come here to ensure that Sin and I had enough supplies for a long trip, but I couldn't stand to see a horse in pain. The supplies would have to wait.

Chapter Four

I checked each weapon and bandage yet again as I waited for one of the horsemaster's pages to hurry off and fetch Sin. I had sent her off to the horsemaster once we had finished with Laith's gelding, with orders to ensure that she was ready for a long journey. Her own shoulder had been injured as well, although the tiny scrape from the arrow was nothing compared to the deep wound that bisected my magical tattoo; I still had no idea what that would do to the enchantment.

The best way to hide a secret was in full view. There had always been rumors that the War Queen had a powerful mage hidden away. This particular story was true, but missing pieces. You see, this powerful mage was also the bearer of a curse, one in which she could only do a magic working when a new War Queen came into power. The new War Queen would choose a War Lady to be tattooed with enchanted ink, the mark powerfully spelled to warn her of danger. It was an honor to be chosen, the mage said, but I hadn't seen it that way. A young girl only just becoming used to my elevated status as a War Lady, still haunted from my past, suddenly asked to become the

Queen's chosen warrior? I had wanted no part of it. Unfortunately, what I wanted had not been taken into account; even now I held the tiniest of grudges for the force that had been used against me in order to place the tattoo, but I couldn't really blame Geneva. At that time, I had been the only War Lady she felt she could trust, since she believed that all of the others had been poisoned by the previous Queen's awful stories. I had mostly forgiven her, due in large part to how many times it had saved my life or another's. The thought of the mark suddenly being stripped from me, or at least stripped of its magic, was as jarring as the thought of getting it had been in the first place.

The page was hurrying back into sight, Sin all but plowing into his back. I snorted quietly. Her excellent ground manners, as usual. The pair had not quite reached me when a shadow fell over me. I spun on my heel, hand resting on my sword, but I was too slow to break the circle. Several War Ladies closed ranks around me, bristling with weapons and temper. My spine was ramrod straight, my knuckles white as I gripped my weapons.

"You aren't going to stay for the ceremony?" Laith asked softly, her doe brown eyes glittering with sadness and hurt. Behind her, the others' faces were less hurt and more accusing. My hand was still tight on the hilt of my sword, so tight that the stitches yanked taut and made me swallow a pained wince. Only just now had I realized what the cut on my hand was from. Sin's rapid halt had ripped the reins through my hands; the thick leather had cut the tender skin of my left palm only, since my right hand had been resting on the hilt of the dagger at the small of my back just as it was now. I didn't really fear any of the other War Ladies, but we were notorious hot bloods. I wouldn't put it past any of them to draw a blade on me when riled, especially with Eili's death so raw. It wouldn't be the first time, or the last.

"I can't," I told her quietly, torn. I was genuinely sorry for the pain it caused Laith, always the kindest and gentlest of us, but I was not sad that I would be missing yet another funeral procession. I had already seen enough of them to last me a lifetime, and no doubt would see many more. It was the way of the world, especially in my profession.

"And why not?" Cian demanded. She stood firmly, feet planted shoulder length apart and hands tight on her wide hips. On anyone else, it would have been the pose of a woman in the midst of a tantrum. On her, it was the look of someone about to draw the hunting knives strapped to each hip. I lifted my chin to meet her challenge, glimpsing the page I had sent off to fetch Sin, hovering, or more accurately cowering, in the background. His grip on her reins was white knuckled, whether from fear of the women who probably terrified him or the powerful mount practically stepping on him to get to me. I waved him forward. He took care to skirt around Cian, risking holding onto Sin for a few moments longer rather than risk Cian's wrath. She was nothing if not vicious, and I wouldn't want him to be hurt by her ire. I shifted forward slightly, just enough to keep Cian's attention on me and not on the child. It was likely that if Cian went after him, Sin would protect him as she had been trained, and then it would really be a problem. I took the reins and shooed him away, never once taking my eyes off Cian.

"Because I am following my Queen's orders, as I am so often shouted at for not doing," I shot back, arching an eyebrow and glaring pointedly at her. Cian was doggedly loyal to anyone who gained her trust, especially her superiors. I was loyal as well, but not blindly so, often punished for disobeying orders when it suited me, or so it seemed. She appeared taken aback that I had thrown it in her face; I jumped on the opportunity. "And not confronting someone about something they can't control."

As a matter of fact, I did have some small amount of control over my situation. I could have petitioned the War Queen for more time, and even if she had refused, I was no stranger to breaking the rules. I could take whatever punishment she doled out, but I wasn't willing to take a whipping to see a funeral, especially since my guilt was already taking care of that task just fine. Not only had I sent Eili to the front, I had forced her to deal with irritating children when she hadn't wanted to. The last thing that I had done was cause her annoyance, which hurt almost as much as the knowledge that it could have been me being laid out on the slab.

Sin chomped on the round bit, tossing her head with impatience to be gone. I stroked her silky muzzle gently, standing quiet in the face of the furious glares. Geneva had ordered me to remain here in the camp until she had composed a missive to the King of Mareen, explaining the plan. I waited outside her tent, struggling to seem unaffected as nearly everyone in the camp took advantage of my open position to glare at me, their eyes filled with unconcealed hostility. Ellis pressed my shoulder comfortingly as he passed, but there was nothing that he could do. Any power he had came from Geneva, and as she was busy in her tent, there was no support to be had. I smiled thankfully at him and turned away, pretending to fix the saddle straps. A soft, shy touch made me spin around, ready for an attack, but I immediately felt bad as the page recoiled, holding a scroll out like a peace offering. I smiled reassuringly, but he ran off before I could apologize, weaving between the hastily erected tents of the camp. I stuck the scroll in my saddlebag and swung into the saddle once I had made sure that the flap of the saddle bag was tightly closed. I could feel glares boring hotly into my back, but I didn't turn around. No War Lady, no matter how riled her temper, would ever stab me in the back. There would be a price to pay when I returned. If only I had known what it was.

Chapter Five

I knew the instant that I crossed the border into Mareen. It was
the moment when a woman with a sword and dagger went from
commonplace to downright profane. In my own country, an
armed woman was taken just as seriously as a man, and anyone
who recognized the fleur de lis symbol on my arm would bow
low. The fact that I wore the uniform was enough to make make
them respect me, even without knowing that I was the War
Queen's chosen champion. Once I crossed the border, however,
what I was wearing earned me too many stares to be borne. I
couldn't draw so much attention to myself. Despite how much I
wanted to stay as I was, ride into a neighboring kingdom with
what pride I could muster half-hunched in the saddle from the
pain, I didn't dare. This was a quiet mission, and my arrival was
anything but. I had to do something about it.

I pulled Sin to the side of the path and led her into a grove
of trees. My knees cracked as I dismounted, making me wince
and flex my long legs in an attempt to rid them of the tailor's
pins that seemed to be stuck in every joint. My fingers, stiff
from gripping the reins so tightly, fumbled with the polished

silver buckles that held my sword belts in place. They hung low across my hips, forming a sort of X just below the small of my back. From one hung the slender length of my silver rapier and a slim dagger with a sapphire in the hilt, a gift from Geneva; from the other, a pistol, the wooden barrel and accents intricately carved. Cool mail covered my torso all the way to the middle of my thighs, with dark pants beneath. A bright blue fleur-de-lis was visible on the left shoulder of my long black cloak, a twin to the enchanted tattoo beneath it. It was all perfectly fitted to my body, hugging every curve like a second skin. It was also surprisingly comfortable, which was just one of the reasons why I was so reluctant to change out of it, but I had to. Otherwise I would stand out too much in this land where women were expected to pick up weapons only when their homes or families were threatened. Sin stood perfectly still in front of me, making a sort of screen while I dragged a different set of clothes out of my saddlebags and stripped down.

Rather than my chain mail, I pulled on a cream corset top, the edges embroidered with lace and velvet roses. My tight leather trousers were replaced with flowing black leggings. From a distance, it seemed to be a skirt, but it gave me the freedom of movement of pants. After replacing my clothing in the saddlebags and closing the buckles, I swung back up and pointed Sin's head toward the nearest small town.

I tucked my chin against the stares, flipping my braid forward and contemplating whether I should take it down to make a better screen. The more small towns that I had to ride through, the better the chance that news of my arrival would spread to the king's spymaster, and from there who knew who else. That was a risk I preferred not to take. Like other towns throughout the kingdom, this one had a sort of signpost at the edge of town, where a weather beaten map flipped sadly in the wind. Sin nosed it curiously, snorting. I pressed it flat against the pole with my fingertips so that it was easier to read. If I pushed it I could make the castle in the next day or two, but I would still have to stop for the night soon. I glanced down at Sin. Her eyes were still bright and alert, but her head nudged toward the ground and her deep chest was flecked with sweat. There was no reason to push her if it would be the next day regardless, so I decided to call it a day.

The sun was low in the sky as I led Sin through town, toward a tall brick building with a welcoming white sign out front. There was a hitching rail out front, but that was for the nightly patrons to leave their mounts while they gambled and drank away their coin inside. The clean, cobbled path led straight to the post, thus eliminating any chance that the drunkards would find themselves lost. The whole of the main street seemed to be designed so that none of the rowdier denizens would find their way into the path of the respectable. There were no houses here, only a few stores and a signpost like the one I had seen earlier. We swung around to the rear of the brick building, where a lush green pasture bordered a courtyard. A ring of stalls curved around the edge; a tower of golden hay bales was planted in the corner. Sin's hooves clicked on the paved courtyard stones.

There didn't seem to be anyone around to ask, so I pulled open the half door to a stall and led Sin inside. The bed of straw was thick and plush; Sin nosed it with her muzzle, dotted with white flecks of sweat. Her saddle came off first, placed on the rack that protruded from the wall, with the thick saddle pad tucked beneath it. Then her bridle. I flung the double reins over her head and loosened the buckles, sliding the headstall over her ears and pulling her thick, curly forelock out of the way so that it didn't get snagged. Finished with that, I turned out of the stall to find her some oats, reflexively reaching for the sword that no longer hung at my waist as I came face to face with a stable boy.

My hand encountered empty air and I slid it around to the small of my back, where the hilt of a tiny dagger protruded ever so slightly from beneath my corset. The boy watched me quietly, his tan face freckled. He didn't seem concerned that I had been reaching for a weapon to run him through with, although only an imbecile would have been able to mistake the gesture for anything other than what it was.

"I ain't never seen no noble take care of their own beast like that. Usually they just pass 'em off to me and don't think no more about it 'til they gotta leave." The boy sounded impressed, or at least I thought so; his thick accent made it difficult to tell.

I hesitated. The fact that he had picked me out as a noble, or what passed for one out here, was worrying. My tattoo remained dormant, without even the barest twinge to indicate that he posed any danger to me, which only corroborated what my own instincts told me. I slowly released the hilt of my dagger, my mind grasping for a way to discover what he knew about me without making him even more suspicious.

"What makes you think that I am a noble?" I hedged.

He shrugged, the flaming red locks that brushed his shoulders swishing with the movement. "You just have that way about you. Like you're used to your orders being followed without question."

I grimaced and shrank a little. I could change my clothes and pull my hair down, try everything I could to seem like every other woman in this kingdom, but there was nothing I could do about my bearing. I dug around in my saddlebags. My long fingers closed around my purse, plump and jangling with coins. By feel I sought out the large gold coin that had the most value, the one that our two countries shared in terms of currency, although the image stamped on them was different. Geneva's face was stamped on this one, wrought in gold that flashed in my palm as I extended it to the boy. "Will this keep you from telling anyone about me?" I asked. I rarely bribed anyone and was unfamiliar with the correct way to do it; most of the time I didn't have to. Either they were afraid of me or they wanted to fight, in which case I obliged them. Rarely was someone ever so little of a threat to me or my mission that I chose to bribe them into silence.

To my surprise, the boy waved away the coin, green eyes flashing with something I couldn't name. "Keep it," he said, eyes alight. "Any noble lady that takes the time to care for a fine beast like that has my silence. You could be inside eating a hot meal, but instead you are out here, taking care of your mount. That's rare."

I flushed and bowed my head at the unexpected praise, all the more of a surprise because I didn't feel that my actions warranted it. It hadn't even occurred to me to pass Sin off and head inside. She carried me around all day, not to mention all of the times she had saved my back. I cared for her because she was my friend. It would be disrespectful to her to pass her off like an unwanted burden.

Everyone around me had a motive. Some feared me, while others wanted to use me as a pedestal to gain status. Only animals were immune to politics.

"Thank you," I said quietly, truly meaning it. The boy seemed to sense my longing to be alone, but at my request, he returned with a kit of grooming tools and a wooden bucket of oats. His eyes dropped to my corset as he hung the bucket from a peg inside the stall; I arched a brow and he backed hurriedly out. I dropped the kit onto a low three legged stool I had dragged in from the outer aisle, grabbed a brush from the kit, and set to cleaning away the sweat and grime of today's adventures from Sin's shining black coat. It was a quiet time for the both of us to relax and unwind, at least until she heard something before I did.

Sin plunged, rising onto her hind legs with a furious whinny. A spark of pain shot through my shoulder, as different from the dull throb of the wound as Sin's ebony form was from that of the snowy white stallion tethered in the yard. I pushed through the pain and spun, drawing my dagger and holding it steady in my left hand. A long rapier glittered in a man's hand, but the shine was nothing compared to the sly smile that graced his full lips. He tossed his head, throwing back the golden hair that slithered over his eyes, a soft moss green with golden flecks. His hand was steady on the sword, his stance easy and even. I stayed in a ready stance, muscles tensed, as Sin rose again behind me. Her flailing hooves cracked against the wooden walls of the stall, making me twitch despite myself. His rapier slid back into its sheath, but I had no illusions that the action meant that he was any less dangerous.

"Milady," the man said slowly, the word sliding off his tongue like honey. He lowered his head in a mocking salute, that mane of gold rippling over his ears and caressing his high cheekbones. "You are not what I expected."

"And what did you expect?" I said sharply. My shoulder's steady throb of warning was going to my head; all I could think of was Geneva's warning, that the mission had been blown before I had even set off. Nevertheless, it rankled that I was still a full day's ride from the palace when my adversaries caught up to me. Perhaps I was losing my touch after all, the fervent hope of every War Lady candidate of the coming year. I wasn't often challenged; people didn't know why I was so strange, because I didn't exactly want to announce my enchanted tattoo to the world, but they knew something was different about me.

Eili... I swallowed hard, thinking about it. Eili had always been the kindest of us. People often mistook kindness for weakness, so all the new fighters looking to gain the title of War Lady had challenged Eili. She was the prime example of how being kind did not mean that one couldn't be a great fighter. Kindness and fierceness had coexisted in her. They had been her greatest strengths, and one of those might have gotten her killed. I gritted my teeth in pain as the man spoke again.

"Something more action appropriate, for one thing," he observed, running his eyes appreciatively over my attire. My hand tightened on the dagger and I stepped toward him deliberately, forcing him to back away or run into the tip. He stepped back, although his arrogant expression suggested that he was humoring me. I reached toward my saddle bag without taking my eyes from him, my rapier producing a satisfying rasp as I drew it from its sheath. It glinted in the light, the silver a contrast to the gold blade that he wielded. His eyebrows arched appreciatively, and he bowed his head once in approval.

"My mistake. You are the Lady Tara, come to speak to my King?"

I hesitated once again. If he meant to aid me, I could hardly turn down the assistance, but if he didn't, then I would be signing the King's death warrant, and my own. Sin's warning and that of the tattoo made me wary, but I didn't have a choice.

"Just Tara. Being called a Lady makes me twitch. And who are you?"

"The King's left hand." He reached out like he might kiss my hand, then dropped it when he realized that both hands were currently occupied with weapons. I didn't move to change that, either. "Loxxley. When will you be ready to head for the castle?"

I sighed darkly and glanced back at Sin, who had her muzzle buried in the oats, ears pricked; the expression was clear. She was still wary of the stranger, but too hungry to care at the moment. My own stomach rumbled with agreement. If I fell out of the saddle from hunger it wouldn't improve the trip, but I couldn't see wasting any more time. Loxxley made the decision for me, glancing at the inn longingly.

"I need a meal before we set out. Would you care to join me?"

I glanced at him, surprised by his seeming vulnerability in the face of his earlier arrogance. Perhaps, like me, what people saw was not who he was. "I would."

Chapter Six

The two of us set out for the palace early the next day. By the time Loxxley and I had finished our meal the night before, it had been too late to attempt to ride any further. Riding in the dark was a dangerous proposition, not only because of the possibility that the horses would injure themselves on some obstacle that they couldn't see in the dark, but also because it would be more difficult for us to spot a threat without the sun. Staying overnight at the inn was an unfortunate necessity.

Setting out in the morning the horses had had a minor disagreement, by which I meant that Sin had refused to come anywhere near Loxxley's white stallion and had taken every opportunity to kick out at him. Once we were again on our way, they settled, but there were a few dicey moments.

Sin's hooves drummed on the dirt, her ears pointed eagerly forward. Loxxley's white stallion moved easily with her, neither of them breathing unduly hard at the steady canter. The silver lion head on Sin's breast band flashed in the soft sunlight. The steady rocking motion and the jingle of tack lulled me into a near stupor; I glanced over at Loxxley. His face, too, was filled with the quiet joy of a good ride. Without consulting one another, we asked our mounts for more speed, which they gave happily, speeding us in our travels.

As if two days of hard riding in uncomfortable clothes wasn't enough, the skies poured rain on us just as the capital city came into view. The horses shied as thunder sounded and lightning shattered the darkness like lines in a dropped mirror. I shivered beneath my sopping cloak, pulling the hood further over my head in the hopes of keeping the freezing, driving rain off my face. The silky strands of hair that had escaped my braid curved limply against my face. Droplets of rain slipped down my face, making me blink as the liquid tangled in my long lashes. I glanced up once, at the city, and then looked down, trusting Loxxley to take me there. I could trust him to do that at least, or so I hoped.

The gates of the city were thrown wide, streams of people slogging through the mud and drizzling rain through them. I guided Sin into place at the rear of the column, but Loxxley shook his head at me.

"We don't wait," he said, like I was some country bumpkin who needed everything explained to her. Sin pinned her ears and bared her teeth at the stallion, which was exactly how I felt toward his rider. Loxxley pulled ahead, using a combination of shouting and quick slaps of a riding crop to part the path. Sin stood perfectly still as I stared in mute horror. A hand grabbed the pommel of Sin's saddle and she jerked, but within a the span of a moment the hand had been transferred to my wrist, her fingers digging into the delicate tendons. The woman's eyes were pleading.

"Please. I need help. My boy is trapped. No one will help. Please, my lady!" Her voice rose at the end, tinged with desper-ation. She looked sincere; no one could fake that amount of panic. Or perhaps it was my natural instinct to help a desperate woman and her child. Either way...

"I'll help," I promised, nudging Sin into motion. Her thick tail swished as she collected herself to turn in a tight circle in the press of the crowd, but before we could follow the woman, a riding crop descended between us; the woman cried out, clutching her shoulder. Loxxley raised the crop for another blow, his face cold and hard as a statue in the square. I glared at him furiously. Before I could think about it, my hand shot out, the crop raising a pink welt on the exposed skin above my bandage where it connected. I twisted my hand around and ripped it from his grasp, getting as close to his face as I could while the horses plunged. "If you don't want to help, don't. Begone."

"You are here to see the King," he said tightly. "Not help some bumpkin who is likely lying to you anyway. All she wants is your coin."

A spark of fury lit through my body. "I am here to do what *I* choose, not you. Do not presume to tell me what that may be. That is not your place."

He stared at me, his face hard, and let out a snort. "Fine. But don't come crying to me when someone ambushes you or steals your purse. I'll be waiting at the palace with the King, whenever you decide to grace us with your presence." Without a backward glance, he spurred the white stallion through the crowd, the shouts of anger even louder this time. I glanced down at the woman, then at the full crowd, and at the area where we needed to go. Just to the left was a dark, abandoned alley. If the layout of this city made any sense whatsoever, then we could go into the dark alley and figure out a way across. Resolved in my decision, I shoved my hand toward the woman. When she didn't move, I sighed impatiently.

"Get on. It will be faster this way." That was all the encouragement she needed. She grasped my injured hand tightly, making me wince, and with my help, managed to clamber clumsily onto Sin's back. Sin didn't care for that, ears pinned flat and legs stiff. Her head lowered toward the cobbles, not like she was tired, but more like she was going to buck. A soft tug on the reins and she raised her head with a huff. I looked over my shoulder at the woman as she clamped her arms around my stomach. "You will have to tell me where we're going." She pointed, and we were off.

Chapter Seven

The woman's name was Marena. This she murmured in my ear only reluctantly when asked, clearly more interested in getting to her son. I could feel her short fingernails raking anxious trails in the skin of my stomach each time she tightened her grip, but I didn't have the heart to say anything to stop her; if that was comfort for her, I could allow her that much. Sin used her broad chest to plough through the crush until there was no crowd, which made progress all the faster. The buildings in this section of the city were dilapidated, the crumbling stone curving in odd directions like the walls were closing in. Marena pointed to an alley and we headed down it, only to discover that Sin's chest was too broad to fit into it. She backed out and I jumped down, flexing my knees to absorb the impact before turning back to help Marena off. She took my hand and swung herself down, albeit with less grace as she stumbled over her plain dress. I went to Sin's head, hooking my fingers through the side of her bridle.

"Stay here," I whispered. Her ears twitched forward and she tossed her head, forelock flipping. I slid past her, the rough stone of the wall scraping my back, and headed down the alley, Marena taking the lead so that she could point the way. Her steps quickened as we reached the end of the row, her tattered skirt snapping around her ankles. The door to the building hung loosely off of its hinges, tilted sideways like a drunkard easing himself down to the ground. Reflexively my hand went to where the hilt of my sword would be, but this morning I had decided not to wear my uniform, choosing instead to wear a dress in order to blend in with the commoners. The beautiful green velvet, cinched tightly at my waist with a braided golden cord, was a little too high class to blend in with the commoners, but even so, no one would have borne me wearing a sword with it. The long, flowing sleeves hid two short daggers, one strapped to each wrist. It made me uncomfortable to be without my sword, especially as my tattoo prickled a warning, but I didn't have time to turn around to get it. I followed Marena through the door, trying to shrug off my feelings of foreboding.

I squinted into the darkness, my eyes struggling to adjust to the lack of light. The falling building might once have been some sort of factory, long trestle tables tilted onto their sides with metal spilled onto the floor, glinting against the stone. It seemed that whomever had once worked here had up and left, but ominous char marks on the far wall and twisted metal told a more sinister story. Goose flesh prickled over my arms and I rocked both wrists forward in an odd jerking motion, one that loosened the daggers in their sheaths and made them much more easy to draw. The windows high above were partially shattered, translucent paper flapping with each gust. I glanced over at Marena. She clutched her arms to her chest and hugged herself tightly, as if she were cold. Or, I thought with a vague sense of alarm, like she was afraid.

"Where is your son?" I asked softly. My hands turned inward to grasp the hilts of the daggers, but I released them as the door banged open with a screaming shriek of protest; unable to take this final act of abuse, it fell outward with a solid thump that raised a cloud of street dust that slowly settled to reveal several men. It wouldn't do to seem too eager to fight, as that was out of the norm for a woman here, but I drew myself up to my full height and tried to look regal, giving them my iciest look. The stable boy had said that I seemed to be a noble; perhaps that act could save me here. The men formed a loose semicircle in front of me, swords drawn. Marena cowered back in the shadows.

"Milady Tara," the leader said mockingly, and my heart sank as his words dispelled any lingering hope that they might be thieves after my purse. It would be a severely unfortunate choice for them, but it would have meant that my identity was safe. Not so. I squinted at the leader, trying to decide if I knew him from somewhere. Bushy sideburns didn't quite hide the jagged scar that ran from beneath his left eye to under his jaw, blunted by a salt and pepper beard. When he smiled, his teeth were black and crooked, making me shudder. The tattered clothes that hung off his broad frame reeked; I could smell them from here. The rest of his goons seemed no better off.

"I don't know what you are talking about," I lied. It slipped smoothly off my tongue, which was odd, because I was a terrible liar. Perhaps that was what happened when one's life was at stake. "You have the wrong woman."

"I don't think so." He pointed at me. For a moment I was confused by what he meant, until I glanced down and swore softly. The shoulder of my dress had slid down the curve of my muscular upper arm, just enough to expose my tattoo. The bright blue of the fleur-de-lis was unmistakable. I sighed darkly and drew my daggers, holding them easily, one in each hand. The bandage on my left hand itched, although it was clean, since I had changed it only this morning. I considered scratching it with the tip of the one of the daggers, but that seemed rather too flippant for the situation. I rubbed it against my belt instead, careful to keep the tip of the dagger pointed away from my thigh. The last thing that I needed was to stab myself before they ever had a chance to.

"Fine. I am who you say I am. What do you want with me?"

The leader seemed a bit taken aback by my forwardness, but he bared his teeth fiercely. "There is someone who needs to see you. Come with us."

"No, thank you," I said politely, like I could just pass on a kidnapping attempt by a group of armed goons. One typically didn't have the option to do such a thing, but when one was me, it was most definitely an option. "I have something to be done yet. Perhaps a bit later. If you give me a way to find them, I'll be happy to stop by a bit later."

The leader lifted the sword and bared his teeth like an animal. I didn't even twitch, and he seemed to take my stillness as hesitation, when in fact it was indifference. Whether they came to me or I went to them, the outcome would be the same. "You will be coming with us. Let us be done."

"Yes, let's," I agreed pleasantly, and then I leapt into action.

There are advantages to fighting in a dress. There must be. However, no matter how hard I search for one, none come to mind. They get stepped on, caught in things, and can be grabbed. In the first few moments of the fight, my dress was stepped on, torn and used to drag me backwards. Finished with that nonsense, I scooped the skirt up as I backed away, then used a dagger to saw the fabric away while the poor fools stared in shock. When I released the wad of velvet, parts fell to the floor and I kicked it away with the heel of one boot. The beautiful dress, which before had dragged nearly to the floor, now hung above my knees. There was quite a bit more air flowing on my bare skin; I spared only a moment to think wryly of what my tailor would say at the destruction before I plunged back into the fight.

My daggers flashed, slithering past the swords extended in my direction. My left hand, already weaker, was even harder to use because of the bulky bandage wrapped around it. This fight needed to end, quickly, and so it did. I slashed with the daggers, then kicked out, the heel of my boot knocking the sword out of his grip. I stepped forward and crossed my daggers at the base of the leader's throat, shooting a glare at the poor fools who had thought to join him. They backed away slowly. I gave a warning shove to the leader.

"Tell whoever you work for that they don't want to meet me. And if you attack me again, I will not be so merciful." I removed the daggers and shoved him away; he staggered to the door, not stopping to retrieve his weapons. I turned to Marena, cringing in the corner, although I did lower my daggers to my side.

"I'm sorry. They made me lead you here. I didn't want to." She cringed back, still clearly terrified. I sighed and sheathed my daggers. This poor woman had been trapped in this situation much more than I had. She didn't deserve my wrath.

"I forgive you." I stalked past her, kicking the fallen door aside. Never again would I be without my sword; fighting with the daggers had made the fight last much longer than it should have. Sin had done as she was told and was waiting at the end of the alley; she backed up reluctantly, providing me with just enough space to climb into the saddle. Her hooves clicked as I turned her toward the castle in the distance. It was a beautiful castle, but I sighed nevertheless. Loxxley would be waiting and I didn't want to hear one word about how I had been betrayed. That was not a good way to start a relationship with a new King.

Chapter Eight

"I need to see the King," I announced.

The soldier looked at me with barely a flicker of interest. He stood stiffly at the entrance to the gates, a pike held upright at his side. He looked exhausted and cranky; I sighed inwardly. Both of those things would make him a joy to deal with. I was right.

The guard scoffed. "And I need to visit a tavern," he shot back. "But neither of those things are going to happen today."

I twisted around in Sin's saddle and dug the missive from my saddle bag, turning the scroll so that the brilliant crimson of the wax behind the War Queen's seal glittered visibly. The guard squinted, but I could tell by his reluctance that he didn't want to allow me entrance.

So help me if I have to scale the wall and drop into the King's very throne room, I will hunt someone down, I thought crossly.

I drew up to my full height, letting the silver filigree hilt of my sword glitter in full view on my left hip and the polished oak of a pistol on my right. "Tell him that the War Queen's emissary has arrived and seeks an audience with His Majesty."

He bristled at being ordered about by a woman. "I challenge you to a duel."

I stared at him, jaw agape. On top of everything else, now this simpleton was challenging me to a duel. I didn't have time for this. "You must be joking."

The blade of his sword chimed as he drew it, holding it in front of him. "You have insulted my honor. In order to prove you are who you say you are, you will have to best me in a duel."

Unbelievable. With an exasperated sigh, I swung out of the saddle, drawing my sword as my feet touched the ground. I would make this quick, for both of our sakes. I didn't want to hurt him, but if he wanted a reprieve from the monotony of guard duty, he was about to get one.

He slashed at my head with a furious shout. I ducked, sliding my dagger from its place on my back and crowding him, nearly jabbing him in the side before he could backpedal enough to give himself some space. Sin clattered out of the way and I slashed half-heartedly, nevertheless shredding his sleeve. There was almost no blood, so I hadn't cut deeply. He hissed and backed away, finally showing some sense that had been absent when he had challenged me in the first place. He didn't have a dagger and our swords were the same length, so I had the advantage.

We circled one another warily. I was fairly certain that I could best him, but I wasn't going to die because of arrogance. He slashed and I ducked out of the way, returning a back-handed stab that barely left him time to block my dagger. He left his left side open when he defended and I could exploit that. I stepped forward, crowding him and feinting toward his right with my sword; he scrambled to defend himself. With my left hand I stabbed with my dagger, sliding it into the filigreed basket hilt of his sword and ripping it out of his hand. He took one step after it before my sword on his throat stopped him cold.

"Do you yield?"

He bowed his head. "Yes, Lady. Forgive me."

I was irritated that I had had to take time out of my day to duel a man that would hardly have had a chance to begin with, but I could understand. All fighters got a little hot under the collar when they didn't have any action for a while; it was only his misfortune that he had chosen a superior fighter to challenge.

"Fool." I raised my head in surprise, curious who had spoken but even more so about how she was referring to. The woman planted her meaty hands on her wide hips and stared me down. Her frilly dress was completely at odds with her bulky frame, a short cap of tawny curls brushing her neck. Shrewd blue eyes squinted at me from beneath pale gold lashes. She rolled her eyes and yanked the poor guard to his feet, shoving him back in the direction of his post; despite the vast differences in their sizes, he went without complaint.

"You are the emissary?" she questioned. She held her hand out expectantly for the scroll, but I wasn't going to give it up to anyone who wasn't a monarch. I compromised by twisting it so that the seal was more clearly visible.

I nodded in response to her question, more emphatically than was strictly necessary. Every moment I wasted was a moment that Eili's killer got further and further away; I had none to waste. "I need to speak with the King," I said, doing my very best to keep my voice neutral and not let any of the urgency that I felt leak into it. I may not have been very successful, as the woman arched a brow. Finally, she nodded, curls bobbing. Skirts swishing as she spun neatly on one heel, she motioned for me to follow her. I shot a filthy glare at the guard who had refused me entrance, which he returned.

I handed Sin off to a waiting stable hand, who led her away immediately, then jogged up the stairs to follow the woman through the palace. Her thick satin skirts swished with each step; I wondered idly how long it had taken to put together that get up this morning, which only made me all the gladder that I didn't have to wear anything other than my uniform, save for those blessedly rare occasions where we War Ladies were paraded about at a ball so that people could see us in all our beauty and ferocity.

The woman stopped so suddenly that I ran into her, her shoulder blunted by the pouf of her puffy sleeves but still sharp enough to make me grunt as it jutted into my collarbone.

"Stay," she ordered, and swished away before I could protest. I arched a brow at her retreating back and made a face, crossing my arms over my chest and seething. It annoyed me to be ordered about like a hound, which might perhaps have been simply because it happened so rarely. Back home, Geneva was the only one who gave me orders with any regularity. Or rather, the only one I chose to listen to.

The guards stood stiffly at attention, staring straight ahead, their faces tight and strained. I knew how they felt. I had been in their position often, but it just so happened that I was far away from anyone with any hold on me. I stood with a hip jutted just outside of the throne room, leg cocked; my hand rested lightly on the hilt of my sword, an old habit I couldn't seem to break. I stared dully at the massive oak doors, iron struts racing down and out. I tucked a loose strand of hair behind my ear and did my best to wait patiently. Beautiful, thick banners draped nearly to the floor, each of them embroidered with various scenes and edged in gold thread.

There was a clatter and a chorus of furious shouts and I spun around, my hand going for a dagger. A gray beast sprinted full speed down the carpet, pursued by a gaggle of hollering servants. I stepped back, but before I could decide what to do, the beast leapt toward me. Only when it skidded to a halt did I realize that what I had thought may be an unholy creature was in fact a dog. Its steel gray coat was long and wildly curly. The legs were oddly long, and yet proportionate to the big, arrow shaped head. Before it could leap on me, I crouched down, putting my face on the same level. The long pink tongue swiped over my mouth and I screwed my face up, clamping my lips closed and secretly glad for the gasp that had pulled air into my lungs. My long fingers sank into the shaggy coat as I grasped for a way to pull the creature away, finally tightening around the band of a thick leather collar. The thick leather held as I pulled the dog down, whispering to it and stroking the narrow head. Behind me, the doors banged open; I shot to my feet in surprise.

A young man glanced down at me, then the dog. He gripped the dog's collar and smiled sheepishly as he dragged the animal back, ignoring its eager whines. The muscles in his forearm strained as he restrained the dog.

"I'm so sorry about him," the man said fervently. His eyes glittered a beautiful blue, crinkling at the corners as he smiled. I had thought he was a man, but he was actually a boy, not much older than I. The lush brown hair that curled slightly at his chin was so thick that it nearly obscured the modest crown nestled at the top of his head. I swallowed hard as I realized that the man who had come bursting out of the throne room in such a hurry to save me from his dog was, in fact, the King. My instinct was not to mention that I knew until he called me on it, but being thrown into the stocks for not showing the King the proper respect would hardly help my case. I hesitated, and before I could come to a decision, the King reached down and took my hand.

My thoughts skidded to a halt as his soft, warm lips pressed gently against the back of my hand. His smile was infectious, and so, despite my blush, I grinned back. He hadn't released my hand, but I decided to ignore that for now.

"I'm Luka," he said quietly. The long strands of his hair fell over his startling blue eyes and he tossed his head impatiently, knocking the crown askew. I swallowed a laugh.

"Tara." I removed my hand from the hilt of my sword to brush my hair nervously out of my face. Those startling blues dropped to the hilt and he opened his mouth, but before he could speak, the woman who had escorted me in puffed up carrying a silver tray.

"Honestly, My Lord," she began tiredly, glaring at me as if I was at fault. "How do you expect to inspire your subjects if they don't even use your title?"

Luka hesitated, then drew himself up, drawing his dignity up like a cloak. "But you're not one of my subjects, are you?" he asked knowingly. The glance at my sword confirmed what both of us already knew, and the woman seemed somewhat mollified. Luka poked his head back into the throne room and to my shock ordered everyone out. At a gesture, I followed him in, dodging the grumbling petitioners and guards who weren't sure whether or not they had been included in those dismissed until Luka motioned again. One stopped, throwing me a filthy look. I glared back, instantly riled at this know-nothing who had never met me and yet chose to judge me.

"Are you certain that this is wise, My Lord?" he asked carefully. "Leaving you with no protection against," he stopped to look at me, his lip curling disdainfully. "Her."

Luka pressed his lips together so tightly that they turned white. "People seem to forget that I fought my way up to this position. I am not helpless. Besides, I'm certain that if Tara had meant me any harm, she would have killed me when I came out to rescue her from Rupert." He placed special emphasis on my name, and his voice was tight, which surprised me. So far I had only seen a quiet, happy go lucky young man, but like everyone else, it seemed that Luka had a dark side. He was correct when he assumed that I could have killed him, but given how calm he appeared at having found a female fighter from another kingdom playing with his dog outside the throne room, no accusations of spying whatsoever, I was inclined to believe that he had at least a fuzzy outline of Geneva's plan. It was a refreshing change of pace.

"Your King is correct. If I had wished harm on him, I would have done something about it before you even looked my way. Besides," I sidled toward him, flashing my strong teeth in a fierce grin. "If I wanted to hurt him, there is absolutely nothing that you could do about it. So go." I shooed him toward the door. His glare could have scorched stone, but he went at a nod from Luka.

"Follow me."

Luka led me to through the throne room. A long, red velvet carpet meandered through the middle of a vast hall, the arched ceiling soaring up so that I had to tilt my head all the way back in order to see the apex; my stiff neck cracked, easing some of the pressure, an unintended but not unwelcome side effect. Massive stained glass windows glittered and cast colored light at our feet, turning the shining marble not covered by the rug into a sea of red, green, blue, purple, yellow, orange, and any combination thereof. It was breathtaking, but I was lagging behind Luka due to my staring.

I hurried to catch up with him where he waited patiently. I must have seemed a country bumpkin to him; my cheeks flamed. He smiled softly at me and led me onto the raised dais, reaching back a hand to help me up. I didn't take it, but he didn't seem offended, just moved on past the throne, a magnificent red oak chair with a high back and seat covered by plush red velvet. A large, luxurious velvet pillow lay on the floor next to the throne. Rupert, the massive gray creature who had followed us thus far from outside the throne room, flopped down and curled up with a contented grunt. I couldn't help but smile.

I was, however, a bit confused as to our destination. Luka seemed to have led us to a solid wall, with no door in sight. He stood in front of a huge tapestry, a scene of knights, dragons, and unicorns, so beautifully woven that it seemed the battle could resume right here in the throne room. I touched the gold thread that it was edged in gently with my fingertips. Something in the bottom right corner of the tapestry caught my eye and I crouched to take a better look, very aware that Luka waited just behind my left shoulder. He knelt down to join me with a pained wince, folding his long legs neatly beneath him and leaning forward so that his chin nearly rested on my shoulder. I glanced back.

"Is that…" I trailed off. Sure enough, outlined in a color so close to that of the background that it could hardly be seen, was a fleur de lis. I touched it lightly with my fingers, startled to feel fingertips on my shoulder.

"It's here, too, isn't it?" Luka said quietly, his long fingers brushing my shoulder, so gently that pain from the touch didn't register. I frowned, my eyebrows drawing together. There was no way he could have known. The top that I was wearing covered my shoulder completely, and even if it hadn't, the wound was still bandaged. While what I was wearing did have a fleur de lis on it, there was no way for him to know that it was also tattooed on my shoulder. That was a closely guarded secret, and hardly anyone knew about it outside of the War Queen's inner circle, let alone a foreign king.

Luka saw my face and shook his head, smiling gently. "I know the legends. If a queen with a fighter who can sense danger is going to have a king brought to her, how much sense would it make for her not to send that fighter?"

I bit my lip, trying to decide whether to confirm what he clearly already knew. My tattoo hadn't warned me of danger from him, which only corroborated my own instincts. I decided to take a risk and nodded slowly. Loosening my sword belt enough that I could slide it off, I peeled off the small jacket that covered my shirt and the bandage around my shoulder. Pulling the shirt down enough that I could unwrap the bandage was a tricky affair; I shot Luka a glance. He watched with only polite interest and looked away the moment I glanced at him. Since I had changed the bandage only this morning, it peeled away cleanly, with none of the dried crust of blood that the previous days' unwrapping had brought. Nevertheless, the area around my tattoo was red and inflamed, the black outline of the mark barely visible with the ugly bruising. Not the best that it had ever looked, but there was no doubt as to the symbol.

Luka reached out, like he was going to touch it, then pulled away. "Follow me." He pulled the tapestry aside. To my shock, what should have been a blank gray wall was actually a door. His long fingers gripped the round golden knob and twisted, pulling it open and motioning for me to enter first. I did, keeping my hand on my sword warily as I stepped into the darkness. Long, dark curtains were partially peeled open so that a scant amount of natural light was admitted. A dark writing desk in the center of the room was filled with papers, a pool of maroon wax congealing on the hard surface. Papers were strewn about on the floor, piles of torn and ink stained, illegible pages. At first, I thought that Luka was merely a terrible house-keeper, that the disarray within was only his way. When I glanced back, however, the tightness of his face warned me that this wasn't the norm.

"What happened here?" I asked quietly. The bandage from

my shoulder was still wrapped loosely around my left hand, already bulky from its own bandages. I transferred the loose bandages to my other hand and used them to pick up the nub of a candle, still warm enough that the melted wax fell over my fingers. I shook it off and winced, extending it to Luka. He took it and set it down.

"It happened again," he said softly, more to himself than me. My head snapped sharply toward him, and he shook his head as he returned to himself. "This is the third time that my office has been raided. Each time, I post more guards and tighten security, and each time, the culprit escapes." He slammed his fist onto the desk in frustration; I jumped, startled by the sudden fury, which was gone nearly as soon as it had come. "I can only imagine that whoever he is must know about this ruse. It may be doomed before we ever set out."

I swallowed, debating whether I should tell him that it was already compromised on my end. Surprisingly, my good sense won out, and I didn't mention it. It was a rare occasion. "I will do my utmost to see you safely to Gen- the War Queen," I vowed, making a face as I caught myself yet again. That promise, at least, was one that I could keep.

Chapter Nine

Sin bared her teeth and kicked out at the gray intruding on her space. I almost felt bad for the gelding, not only because he had very nearly gotten kicked in the chops, but because of the man on his back. It was the guard who had tried to convince Luka to keep me out of the throne room yesterday, and I liked him even less now that I had spent these past hours in his presence. He seemed determined to hold a grudge against me for putting him in his place yesterday, and I was just as determined to hold one for his attitude. The poor gelding was snorting wildly and doing his very best to get away from Sin, who had her ears pinned flat, but the angry guard would not let him back away. I snapped the reins lightly at Sin and urged her forward to Luka's side, giving the little gray a bit of much needed space.

"How are you doing?" Luka inquired. He rode at the head of the caravan, which as a leader was both admirable and foolhardy. It meant that while he did look good out in front of his group, he also lacked the protection of being surrounded by guards. I resolved to stay by his side as much as I could. So long as the horses allowed, which, so far, seemed likely. Loxxley rode on the other side of Luka; their white stallions seemed to blend into one if I didn't look very carefully. Sin stretched out her neck toward Luka's mount and I tensed, tightening my grip on the reins in case I needed to pull her away before things got ugly. Instead, she touched muzzles lightly and then pulled away like nothing had happened. Luka and I both relaxed in our saddles and breathed identical sighs of relief, which reminded me that I had yet to answer the question he had asked me.

"Fine," I said honestly. I rolled my injured shoulder, impressed that the pain was much dulled by how well it had been wrapped. After I had unraveled the bandage to show Luka my tattoo, he had insisted on rebandaging it himself, even doing a surprisingly good job. It was easy to forget, with his easy going demeanor and gentle eyes, that he had fought his way up to this position. And yet, there was something about the way he stood, his lean frame composed into that nonchalant watchfulness that was the trademark of a good swordsman. Or swordswoman. While I had no doubt that he was extremely skilled, I couldn't help but hope that I never had the occasion to see his skills in action. That was the part of me that wanted to return him to Geneva as soon as possible so that I could hunt down Eili's killer. That was the part of me that was winning out, but a smaller part warned that I might enjoy seeing him fight. I tried to ignore it and sent up a prayer to whichever deity might have been in a listening mood that we encountered no more trouble.

Loxxley poked his head around Luka's broad shoulder to glance at me. His hair flipped over one eye and he tossed his head impatiently. "It surprised me when my brother spoke of how you were injured. An arrow?" His full lips pursed, but despite that, I couldn't help but think that his face was eerily similar to someone else's. A quick glance to the side told me that the face was Luka's. They had the same dark eyebrows and sharp, hooked noses. Their hair was a different color, as were their eyes, although they had the same intensity. I couldn't help but study them, even though I knew that I shouldn't. I dragged my gaze away and stared forward, between Sin's black ears. Whether or not the two were related, their striking resemblance meant nothing to me. Luka was my objective, and Loxxley was merely a distraction.

"Yes, an arrow. I and a few of the other War Ladies were meant to be escorting a group of young ladies to a finishing school. On our return, we would resume progress with the War Queen. We were ambushed. One of our number was killed, and I was injured."

We were coming up on a small town, but the main road appeared to be blocked by an overturned wagon. We slowed as we approached, the horses blowing and snorting impatiently. The only roads that headed in the direction we were going were too small to admit us, and would be hard on the horses. Men and women scurried around the wagon, collecting items that I couldn't see even when I squinted. I urged Sin forward so that we were in front, motioning for the caravan to halt. They did, with a great clatter of reins and hooves. Despite my signal for him to wait with the others, Luka joined me, followed closely by Loxxley. I sighed darkly and rolled my eyes, flinging my right leg across the front of my saddle and scooting off. It was most definitely not the typical way to dismount, nor the most graceful, but it was how I did it. Luka swung out of the saddle and stepped as close as Sin would allow, peeking around her dark head and stroking her cheek with the hand that wasn't holding his own mount's reins. It was a casual, nonchalant motion, like showing fondness to an animal not his own was second nature. I shouldn't have been surprised, but it it did warm my heart a little. I patted Sin's neck and dropped her reins, striding forward confidently with my hand braced on the hilt of my sword.

Out of the corner of my eye, I saw Luka lunge for Sin's reins, only to draw up short when he realized that she hadn't moved. Loxxley snorted under his breath and dragged his brother forward after me.

"What is going on here?" I inquired. Several of the people rushing around the wagon glanced up at me, but only one stopped chasing the tiny objects to speak. He straightened slowly from his crouched running position with a strained groan, back cracking. His bushy gray brows poked out from the corners of his flat brown eyes like a feather in a hat. His mouth was turned down and surrounded by deep wrinkles. He frowned at us and crossed his arms, pale white slashes of scars bulging on his forearms. Almost without thinking about it, I rubbed the tender skin of my right wrist, on the side not on the silver hilt of my sword, against the heavy leather of my jacket. I had scars like his, perfectly straight lines just below the heel of my hand, five gashes that made my heart hurt every time I looked at them. They were a memory of a time in my life when I had not been in the best place, but without times like that, I wouldn't be who I was today. I wasn't ashamed of them, only saddened.

"What do you want?" the man snapped. His attitude irritated me. I admit it, after several days spent mostly in the saddle, I wasn't feeling the most rational. My shoulders went rigid and I opened my mouth to knock him down a peg, when a warm hand gripped the back of my elbow. Luka shot me a warning glance.

"We would like only to pass through," he soothed. "If you would let us pass, we would be exceedingly grateful." His chin was lifted, but not in the prideful way that Loxxley's was. Luka's was more like a silent plea for help, and yet somehow, it didn't convey weakness. The man frowned and motioned aggressively for us to wait, turning his back and tromping over to the others. Luka watched quietly. The soft waves of his brown hair slid over the corner of his eye and he ran his hand through it, ruffling it and leaving one lock flipped against the part. My hand had reached out to flip it back into its proper place and he mouthed his thanks at me even as my cheeks flamed. He didn't seem to think that my touching him was anything out of the ordinary, but it was. I never touched anyone, at least not like I wanted to touch him. The only physical contact that I ever had was bandaging someone up or when they did the same to me. I shook my head slightly and edged away from Luka just as the man returned, his mouth pinched into a tight frown.

"We are having difficulties picking this up. You will have to go around if you don't want to be stuck here until it's cleaned up."

I frowned. While I didn't particularly want to be stuck here for however long this would take, I also didn't want to go who knew how far out of our way, on a path that I knew nothing about. This was just as likely a trap as anything else, but I saw no other alternative. I looked to Luka and Loxxley; both of them stared back, with Luka waiting for my recommendation and Loxxley not seeming to care either way; his jaw clicked as he yawned wide as a snake, proving that he wasn't overly concerned about what was happening. Although his breezy attitude irritated me, I figured it would be better that than have him fight me tooth and nail on every decision, which his temperament would definitely allow.

"Would you be able to provide a guide for us? We are unsure of this path, and someone who knows the area would be greatly appreciated. We will pay you, of course." The man hesitated, then raised his voice to call someone over. A young man jogged around the overturned wagon, halting next to the short, pudgy man with the sour face. The young man couldn't have been more than a few years older than Loxxley, who was the oldest of our trio. In fact, he looked a lot like the stable boy who had been so impressed about my caring for Sin, with the same bushy red hair and pale eyebrows. He stared at us for a moment, completely ignoring the man's low grumbles, and then blinked wildly.

"Yes, I would be happy to guide you," he said quietly. I frowned briefly. He had been so intent on staring at the three of us, without once raising his eyes to look at the troop of soldiers behind us or turning his head to acknowledge the man who had called him over, I would have thought that he hadn't even heard him. "Let me saddle my horse and I will meet you here in a few minutes. If you would like to water your animals, there is a well over there where you may refresh yourself." My eyes followed his pointing finger to a brick well, the reddish stone crumbling slightly at the base. From here, I could see that the bucket to be filled with water was reeled up, the rope it was attached to wound around the handle to tether it. It wasn't far away, and my dry throat begged for refreshment, since drinks from our canteens were few and far between in case water sources were sparse. Luka thanked the red haired man and tapped the back of my wrist lightly to get my attention, the horses nearly stepping on us in their anticipation for the water. I couldn't hide a smile.

The rough hemp of the rope bit into the palms of my hands and I winced, looping it around a peg and tying it off before wiping my stinging palms on my pants. They were red and scratched from hauling up the heavy bucket of water, but Luka and Loxxley had already taken their turn at it, and I wasn't about to shirk my duty. Sin plunged her muzzle into the bucket, making impolite slurping sounds and blowing bubbles through her nostrils as she guzzled down the cool liquid. A dented silver ladle had been hung on the well for use, but I ignored it and shoved my hands into the sturdy wooden bucket, pushing Sin's heavy head aside so that I could gather some water into my cupped hands. The liquid was freezing against the back of my throat as I swallowed, but it was unbelievably refreshing. I sighed in ecstasy and stepped aside for the next person to take their turn.

"It's hard to imagine how something as simple as water can taste so good, isn't it?" Luka asked. He was bent over to check his horse's hoof for a stone, the hoof held gently between his palms, but straightened as he spoke. The white stallion nudged him and Luka laughed, stroking his long nose gently.

"Yes, it is," I agreed, my mouth still tingling from the freezing water. My teeth ached from the bitter bite, but my thirst was quenched; I couldn't complain. The other soldiers were just finishing watering their mounts and refilling their water skins when our guide returned. I clicked my fingers together lightly and Sin lifted her head reluctantly from the lush green grass that her muzzle was buried in, trotting to my side. I offered her one more drink from the nearly empty bucket, which she refused.

"Are you ready?" the red haired man inquired. He was already mounted, on a short gray mare who puffed her nostrils out and tossed her head. I swung onto Sin's back, stitches pinching. The others mounted up as well, and we pointed the horses toward the dark forest, which was eerily backed by the setting sun. Little did we know that things were about to get a lot darker.

Chapter Ten

"This has got to stop pretty soon!" I shouted indignantly. Luka nodded, his face alarmingly close to mine where we crouched together. A forest of arrows jutted from the mossy forest floor in front of us, the black shafts the same ones that had been pulled out of my body before. My shoulder twinged, both from the remembered pain and the actual pain from my burning tattoo. My hand went to it of its own volition, fingers contracting around the top of my arm like I could stop the blinding pain that way. Arrows were still falling all around us, but Luka didn't seem to notice. He leaned even closer, his hand placed gently atop mine and the skin around his blue eyes pinched as he watched me in concern. I inhaled deeply through my mouth and exhaled through my nose, concentrating on his hand, his face, anything other than the pain and the fact that if the hail of arrows moved any further in our direction, we might all die today.

"Am I the only one that thinks perhaps our enemies need to work on their aim?" Loxxley said. I snorted, but he was only partially wrong. Our enemies were picking off our guards one by one, and yet they never seemed to get close enough to the three of us to do any real damage. Enough to startle us in a few cases, as with the arrow quivering the tree mere inches from my face that made me scoot back with a startled yelp. Despite the less than opportune circumstances, he didn't seem the slightest bit worried. A miniature crossbow, a scaled down version of the heavy monsters that would normally have been carried, was gripped expertly in his big hands; from what I had seen, he was a good shot with it. He was crouched near Luka and me, back pressed to the broad trunk of a tree. He peered around again and shot off another arrow; there was a scream of pain. Luka and I did the same with our pistols, the crack of the hammers and the dark puff of smoke, illuminated by the sparks, a welcome break from the darkness. The sun was low on the horizon, surrounded by a sky that looked suspiciously like bloody skin, maroon and soft tangerine that nevertheless reminded me of a bullet wound. I winced, and thought about how this had all come about.

The journey into the forest had been uneventful at first, with no real indicators that it would be anything otherwise. The horses were skittish, shying at shadows and the slightest of noises. The tall trees were eerily quiet, leafy green branches whispering in the slight breeze. Flocks of small black birds shot into the sky with a chittering screech; Sin shied, swerving to the side and kicking out with her huge hooves. Luka's white stallion rose into a half-rear. I tensed, expecting him to slide off the massive horse's back. Instead, he crouched close to the arched neck, gripping the thick white mane, and pushed the horse back down to earth. Surprised by the show of horsemanship, I smiled at him, and he grinned back, eyes bright. There was a loud thud behind us and we both twisted in our saddles, then burst out laughing. One of the soldiers in our escort had not been so lucky with staying on his mount and now lay flat on his back, gripping the loose reins tightly so the mare didn't bolt and smiling sheepishly. We laughed for a moment longer as he crawled back into the saddle, but our guide wasn't so understanding. He turned his horse back and rode into the midst of us, his face tight with fear and impatience. My tattoo burned, and all hell broke loose right then and there.

"Watch out!" Arrows fell from the sky like a deadly rain. I shrank down in my saddle and held on for dear life as Sin bolted, leading the other horses in a headlong rush for the cover of the thickest trees. Arrows fell in her path and she swerved, jolting me loose. As if in slow motion, I slid out of the saddle, the ground rushing toward my face. I tucked my shoulder under me and rolled, the hard metal of my weapons digging into my skin. Sin's hooves thudded by my face as she continued on. I had no doubt that she would try to turn around and get back to me, but being caught in a stampede of frantic horses was never a good thing. I covered my head and curled up as tightly as I could, squinting through slitted eyes to see when it was safe to lift my head. I could just see twin flashes of white through the chaos, arrows still falling and the bodies of the soldiers keeling out of their saddles as the horses stampeded. I lifted my head just a bit further and nearly got it taken off by a flying hoof. The two white flashes came closer, and I could see now that they were the white stallions, ridden by Luka and Loxxley. They were both struggling to get back to me, their faces tight with panic. Luka's horse stumbled, and he disappeared from sight.

My heart leapt into my throat as a body fell next to me, reminding me that I would do better to worry about myself. By the time Luka was in sight again, Loxxley had appeared near me, leaning out of his saddle and extending his hand to me. I leapt to my feet and took his hand, using my momentum to swing up behind him. I clung on tightly as we rode for cover, but swung off as soon as we reached a safe spot. The hail of arrows had continued since.

Suddenly, the soft thuds of arrows impaling themselves in deep moss ceased. I poked my head out from the cover of the tree, stopping halfway through cleaning and reloading my pistol. The sky was dark and dotted with gleaming stars, but the forest was blackness itself. Luka glanced at me and cautiously peered out the other side of the tree. We were so close together that I could feel the tightness of his muscles as he moved; I shivered unexpectedly. When Luka shrugged and nodded to indicate that he could see no threat, we all stood cautiously and moved from our hiding places to inspect the carnage.

My heart lurched and I raised my hands to my mouth for only a moment before dropping them again. War Ladies could not show weakness, no matter what, especially to what the War Queen would have considered an enemy, or at the very least an unstable ally. I straightened up and threw my shoulders back, startled by the sudden burn in my shoulder. I dropped like a stone, searching for danger, but there were still no live guards to be found, only the bodies of nearly every soldier and their horse. Only when I touched my shoulder gently with the tips of my fingers did I realize that I had once again torn the stitches in the wound. Crimson blood sparkled against the ebony of my jacket, lit by the soft silver rays of the moon. I wiped the blood on my fingers off on the thick leaf litter, trying not to think how much blood already stained the spiky russet leaves.

Loxxley watched me with a vague sort of fascination, but he made no move toward me. Luka was facing away from me, but he turned to speak to Loxxley and saw me on the ground. His head tilted back sharply in startlement, the silver moonlight sparking off his bright blue eyes. Too late I realized that he had seen me crouched on the ground, surrounded by blood, my hands stained with it. His face whitened, the tanned skin and flushed cheeks leaching of color like wine being spilled on parchment, only in reverse. He rushed toward me, but I held up my hand to stop him, laughing softly at his reaction. So eager was he to follow my signal to stop that he skidded to a halt, freezing mid motion and waiting for permission to come closer. I was glad of it. The events of the night had rattled me, making my heart ache for the soldiers and animals that had died tonight, with nothing to be done to find their murderers. "War Ladies do not show weakness" had been drilled into me so much that I repeated it without thinking in times of stress, but for the first time in a long time, I didn't care. For the first time in a long time, I wanted to be held and comforted. I couldn't let that happen, especially not with Luka, who was the leader of another country, one who may be in trouble with my liege. At the very least, he was far outside my circle of possibilities for companionship. Loxxley, of course, had never been an option.

I dragged myself to my feet with difficulty. A soft whicker made me smile; I didn't even have to look to see which horse it was. Sin poked my bloody shoulder with her muzzle, making me wince. I grasped her bridle and pulled her away from the wound, gently kissing her forehead just above the silver lion of her bridle.

"Good girl," I whispered. "You came back. Just like I knew you would. Like you always do."

Two hands appeared. Both had long, strong fingers. A golden ring glittered on one, with a silver one on the other. I glanced back at the boys, startled to see how close they were. Loxxley looked at Sin with something very like fondness, or the closest that I had seen from him yet. It made him look like Luka, despite the differences in hair and eye colors. Luka smiled at Sin, the corners of his eyes crinkling and the blue sparkling in the light, glinting like the silver ring on the ring finger on his left hand. I was startled by its placement, but I swallowed and stepped back, forcing the boys to step back a bit. As she always did, Sin sensed my feelings, which were at this particular moment somewhere between anxiety and miffed curiosity. Any feelings that I may or may not have been considering careened to a heavy halt that very moment. There was only one reason that I could think of for a ring to be worn on that particular finger, and I wanted less than nothing to do with that.

Sin struck out with her hooves and ripped her head up against my grip on the reins, nearly slamming Luka in the chin with her hard head. I took the excuse to step away and lead her in a slow circle, using her dark body to give me a chance to think. I couldn't help the surge of disappointment that flooded my chest, although I knew I had no right to any feeling of the sort. It was my own fault for getting too attached. I had known very well what I was getting into when Geneva had given me this task. I should never have done anything like this, and I deserved what I got.

"So now what?" Luka said suddenly. He stood by Loxxley, who was holding his white stallion. I searched for Luka's horse, but he was nowhere in sight. He must have bolted during the commotion, although I was certain that I had seen Luka trying to get back to me on his back. Perhaps after that? "What are we going to do now? This is the second suspicious attack in two days, not to mention the ones before. How are we going to reach your Queen safely?"

I rubbed my forehead lightly, trying to figure out what our next step should be. We were at least a day's ride away from Geneva's camp, and by the time I sent a messenger to ask her to come to meet us, it would be too late. These attacks couldn't be random; the timing was too precise to be a coincidence. What I couldn't figure out were the arrows. If these attacks were intended to prevent me from escorting Luka to speak with

Geneva, then why had the first attack been on me, personally? I crouched and pulled an arrow out of the ground by its ominous black fletching, feeling a twinge of remembrance. I loosened the buckle on Sin's saddlebag and dug around until my fingers brushed dry wood. I pinched the arrow between my thumb and pointer finger to pull it out, not bothering to disguise my distaste. The iron tip of the arrow was stained with dried blood. Mine. I made a face at it and held the other up to compare the two, squinting in the moonlight.

A sudden flare of smoky orange and red made me cringe. Loxxley arched one dark, defined eyebrow and held the torch higher, the light spilling over the arrows and my hands. It flickered in the slight breeze and I hunched my shoulders slightly, which made my shoulder ooze blood all the more. I had almost forgotten about it, but it was too late to play it off; Loxxley had already seen it. His eyes dropped to the shoulder of my jacket, to the hastily repaired tear in the black leather from the arrow. There was no new tear, but blood had leaked through the gap and stained it even darker, sliding down my chest in a languid trail. I had a feeling that I should be concerned about the wound, but since this was the third or fourth time I had torn out this particular set of stitches, I just couldn't summon the energy to care, especially after the night we'd had.

"You are bleeding," Loxxley pointed out, like I hadn't already noticed. I gave him a dry look and dug through Sin's saddlebags once again, laying the arrows on the ground so that both hands were free for what I needed to do. A roll of creamy white bandages came out first, along with a short, slender bottle of pale liquid that was carefully corked. I also withdrew a short knife, more suited to a medicinal task than to use as a dagger or other stabbing implement. I hugged it all to my chest and lowered myself onto a log, not caring that I had poked myself in the arm with the blade of the tiny knife. Only after I had shed my jacket and was halfway through unwrapping the bandage around my shoulder did I realize how quiet it was.

The boys were watching me with a sort of startled fascination. Loxxley's arm drooped toward the ground, the torch sputtering and sparking as it neared the leaves.

"What?" I demanded. Luka shook himself, his soft brown hair falling over one eye before he tossed it back. One high cheekbone was scraped in an odd, side to side manner. The hair on the top of his head was ruffled up where his crown had lain; I wondered idly what he had done with it. I hadn't seen him wearing it for most of the trip, and he certainly hadn't been wearing it during any of our battles. Short lived as they may have been, I would have noticed. Not to mention the fact that it defeated the purpose of him traveling incognito if he wore a crown to announce his royal status. Loxxley had handed the torch to Luka and stepped away. I had a sick feeling that I knew what he was doing.

"What do you think you're doing?"

I sighed darkly. "I need medical attention before we continue on. With all the trouble we've been having, I think we should continue riding tonight, but I need these looked at," I motioned to my shoulder and my hand, which had somehow managed to keep its stitches properly. Ironic, since now they needed to come out, sooner rather than later. I knew this, since I knew stitches like the back of my hand. "And you need a horse," I pointed out.

"We'll worry about that later. Right now, you can let someone take care of you for a change." Luka sat next to me and took over unwrapping the bandage. His long fingers skipped lightly over my shoulder with each revolution. The pale blue fleur-de-lis was stained red with blood. Luka took the knife and briskly cut a swath of the bandage apart from the rest, soaking it thoroughly with the clear liquid from the bottle. My grasp tightened on the rough brown bark of the fallen log as he carefully swiped at the blood, so tightly that a sliver of the wood slid painfully under my fingernail. That, however, was nothing compared to the pain of strong alcohol on an open wound.

"How do you know?" I gasped out, trying to take my mind off of what had just happened and what was about to happen. Luka was carefully rinsing the blade of the short knife with the alcohol, sterilizing it before he used it to remove the stitches in my hand and the what was left of the ones in my shoulder.

Luka raised his eyes to mine curiously, the flickering light of the torch and the bright rays of the half moon warring to brighten the light blue. One long sprig of deep brown hair slid over his eye and he tilted his head slightly, his long lashes tangling with the soft lock. I reached up to brush it back, then dropped my hand forcefully into my lap. He followed it with his eyes, then flicked them back up to mine. The soft yet vivid blue was flecked with gray, the opposite of mine, which were stormy gray with splotches of blue like the sky.

"How did I know what?" he asked curiously. He slipped the knife under the mangled stitches and tugged gently, pulling them out one by one. Holding tight to the log was getting me nowhere, so I grabbed the next best thing: him. My strong fingers tightened on his shoulder. His head jerked up, startled, but then he went back to work like nothing had happened. I told myself again and again that it was only for comfort, but I wasn't sure if I believed myself.

"That I never let anyone else take care of me. You don't know that. For all you know, I could be some pampered princess who is waited on hand and foot by an armada of servants," I said stubbornly, breathing deeply through my mouth and holding as still as I could while he drew the last of the stitches in my hand out, but I couldn't help but jolt in surprise as he barked a laugh; the skin pinched and I hurriedly stilled, listening to his laughter. It was deeper and more gravelly than I would have expected from his velvety speaking voice, but somehow it was more *him* than anything else.

"That's not true and we both know it," he chided. "No spoiled little princess would ride days in the rain to meet a man that she's never met and escort him safely to his destination. And," he added, tightening his grip on my injured hand when I tried to pull away, although not enough to hurt. "You wouldn't have stayed. You could have left us at any time, but you stayed, in the middle of a bloody battle, and defended us when you were hurt yourself."

He traced the healing scar on my palm gently with his fingertip. It tickled, and I shivered vigorously, which brought a bright smile to Luka's face before he sobered to work on my mangled shoulder. Once the stitches were out, he stopped, reaching to touch the fleur-de-lis before he dropped his hand, just as he had done before.

"What is it like?" he asked, unrolling a length of clean bandage from the carefully wrapped roll, since we, or rather I, had decided that no more stitches should be put in; they hadn't worked so well before.

"What is what like?" I asked. He tapped the tattoo gently with a finger. "Having this?" I placed my palm lightly over the mark and tilted my head as I considered how best to respond. When I had first gotten it, I would have said bitterly that I hated it, that I would give anything to have it removed. Now, years later, I could only barely see what that version of myself had been saying. I understood the bitterness from the means used to force me into what should have been purely my decision, leveled against me by someone who I had thought was my friend. We had been through alot together, and I had been the only one to back her in her challenge of the previous War Queen, risking both my position and my life. This deed that had forced what I considered an unnatural and unwanted burden on me felt like a betrayal. Now, however, I had calmed down about it. It was difficult to feel bitter over something that had saved my life, as well as the lives of others, so many times. Now I couldn't imagine being without it.

"Strange," I said honestly. "It took some getting used to. It warns me of immediate danger, although occasionally I have trouble discerning what the warning concerns." Almost immediately, I cringed inwardly. Telling him such a secret would have Geneva in fits; it could easily be used against me. It didn't matter, because it was too late now. Luka frowned contemplatively, but nodded and tied off the bandage on my shoulder, hiding the pale blue fleur de lis tattoo.

"Well, it seems like both a blessing and a curse," he observed softly, and that was all he said; I couldn't have agreed more. The torch sputtered and went out. I expected us to be pitched into blackness. However, the moon, which had been so bright earlier, had been replaced with the first rays of the sun, peeking over the horizon. While Luka had been caring for me, Loxxley had removed the bodies of the soldiers, although the still bodies of the dead horses made my eyes burn with tears, my throat aching as though I had swallowed something hard. Something about horses got to me as nothing else did. The soft arch of the rising sun basked in warm reds, rust oranges, and bright yellows. I squinted, surprised by how quickly the night had passed. My long fingers dug into the sides of my biceps as I hugged myself tightly, then pushed myself up from the log, stiff joints cracking audibly. Luka's hand was on my elbow in an instant, lending me support but removing it the moment I indicated that I was fine. I appreciated that.

Loxxley had returned, although without the mud or sweat that I had expected. The long strands of his hair curled damply at his collar, soaking the top of his shirt and leaving beads on the smooth planes of his collarbone. His face was still wet, one clear bead sliding down his chiseled features like a tear. He shook the sleek mane out and strode toward us, offering a bulging waterskin. I accepted it with a grateful nod, almost choking at his next words. I swallowed with difficulty and let out a strained cough that I tried to muffle with my hand. The boys were too preoccupied to notice.

"We're alone. They have weakened us."

"What are you saying?" I asked, even as my heart sank to my bloodstained boots. I knew what he meant; what he said next only confirmed it.

"All of the soldiers are dead. We're the only ones left."

Luka paled, bright spots of anger pinking his high cheek-bones. He tilted his chin down and closed his eyes, long black lashes twining with his hair where it slipped down to touch his face. I wanted to comfort him, but I was too much in shock myself.

"The trap was never for us," I said, more to myself than the boys. Luka opened his mouth to protest, but I ignored him. "It was for them. To show that they could kill whoever they wanted, whenever they wanted, with complete impunity, and without any fear of retribution from us." I reached to touch my shoulder, my face tight with pain. This had all started with that first ambush, with the injury seemingly meant to disrupt the enchantment that no one else should have known of. There were very few who knew of the magic of the tattoo, and even fewer whom I did not trust with my life. The only explanation that I could think of was that the ambush, and such a specific injury as the one that had felled me, were both orchestrated to take me out of commission. The intent had not been the result, so this ambush was meant to scare us into turning back. If that was what the unknown assailants wanted, then that was what we must not do.

Loxxley seemed to reach the conclusion the same moment I did. He jogged to the other end of the clearing to round up the horses, grabbing his horse's reins and reaching for Sin's, wincing and backing away when she kicked out, ears flat and teeth bared. I chuckled softly and whistled piercingly; Sin skirted Loxxley with a look that was almost defiant, slowing to a halt in front of me and tossing her head. She stretched toward Luka, nostrils flared so that the veins were purple rivers in the pale pink lining. I froze, hardly daring to breathe, until she shook her head and turned back to me. Sin never made advances toward anyone else, so it came as a surprise that she would even investigate Luka. That was good; otherwise she would never have let him ride with me.

Chapter Eleven

"Still more than a full day's ride away," Loxxley said grimly, tracing one slender finger over the map laid out across the table. The edges were pinned down by heavy, fist sized rocks. I dipped one finger into a slash from a knife in the heavy wooden table and nodded glumly, rubbing my hands lightly together, the calluses from riding scraping against one another. We had been forced to stop for the night by a storm, the horses too skittish to continue any further in the pounding rain and cracking thunder. Normally they were calmer than that, since they had to be to put up with the constant dangerous situations that we allowed ourselves to be put through in the name of our work. Unfortunately, tonight was not the best night for any of us. The horses were skittish, a show of how nervous we all were, although we humans were too brave or too ashamed to admit it. I could tell that Sin didn't appreciate having a second rider, which would only tire her more quickly. It was never going to be a long arrangement, which we all knew when we left the forest. I, for one, was just glad to be away from the blood and the ghosts of the bodies.

Only luck had it that we had managed to find an inn soon after, and had used some of Luka's inadvisably large stash of coins to buy rooms, meals, and baths, as well as stabling for the two horses of our party. We had not been able to recapture any of the horses that had fled, and with Loxxley's horse injured in the fighting, Luka had ridden with me for most of the day. Every bump and jolt had made us clash against each other; when we stopped for the day, it was both a relief and not. Sin, of course, hated us riding double. Her opinion was clear with her nips and constant pinned ears.

"And who knows how many traps and ambushes could be lying in wait," Luka finished. His broad shoulders were bowed forward, sharp elbows digging into the table and his head lowered. Long strands of hair fell into his face and I twitched with the need to push them back, but if he didn't, nor would I. His slender fingers were wound together and he tightened them so hard that his knuckles whitened, then popped audibly. I tucked a strand of my own hair behind my ear and unwound the long braid that had worked so hard to keep the lush mane contained throughout the long day. It was falling down anyway, but my hair sprang free as soon as it was loosed. I wrapped the leather strap lightly around my wrist and tied it off, glancing up when I noticed the lack of conversation, at least at our table. The boys were staring openly. Luka flushed and glanced away as soon as I looked up, but Loxxley met my eyes calmly and reached out, long fingers skating through my hair. I froze, but he held up a strand of green grass and grinned wickedly. I nodded in thanks and tried to keep my flaming cheeks from catching the table on fire.

"You look different," Luka mumbled. "With your hair down."

I contemplated that. It was an odd thing to think that someone was paying close enough attention to my face to think that it looked different with my hair styled differently. Flattering, but strange.

The conversation at our table had stilled for the moment, but the rest of the dining room was lively. A grizzly old man with a beard that flowed over his ample belly, his nose a thick beak poking over pouchy lips, drank silently in the corner. Five drunken men played a game in another corner, tossing grimy dice onto a table stacked high with coins. A beautiful woman with streaked red hair drank daintily out of a glass tumbler at the bar. A harried barmaid slithered between the crowded tables like an eel, balancing a tray loaded with full pitchers of mead and plates of roasted pig, surrounded by dark greens and bright orange carrots. My stomach rumbled in protest; I clapped my hand over it and flushed, once more staring in apparent fascination at the table so that I didn't have to look at the other two.

Luka grinned at me and waved over the barmaid. She weaved toward us with an exasperated sigh, flipping her head impatiently to toss her black hair back from her face. Her brown eyes were shrewd as she glared down at us with thinly veiled impatience. Loxxley straightened in his chair, running a hand through his hair before folding them carefully on the table.

"If we could order a meal and a drink for the three of us, that would be greatly appreciated," he said smoothly. The woman arched a brow and nodded with barely concealed impatience, deftly sweeping a drunk customer's hand away from her wrist. I tensed, reaching for the dagger strapped to the inside of my wrist, but she swished away without so much as a backward glance. Luka removed his hand from a dagger in the same place on his own wrist, although with his sleeves pushed up the sheath was clearly visible. Loxxley was half-standing, his palms braced on the table. His eyes followed the barmaid as he sank back down.

"Perhaps we should join a game of chance," Luka suggested,

although he looked less than enthusiastic about his own suggestion, his eyes tracing warily over the drunken gamblers. They tossed the bone dice with an aggressiveness that bespoke lots of drinking, occasionally blustering angrily and throwing a punch. As we watched, one of the men tipped another's chair and used it as an excuse to pilfer a few coins from the stack in front of him. By the time his "friend" had managed to right the chair, a task made much more difficult by the drinking he had likely been doing all day long, the thief was firmly seated in his chair with no indication that he had ever been anything other. I rolled my eyes but couldn't help but admire his shrewdness.

Loxxley had left the table; he leaned casually against the bar, his right elbow planted in the only open space on the hard wood, between pitchers and clear glasses of smoky amber liquid. Luka and I took one look at each other, then at the brawling gamblers, and stood to go. We hurried between the tables before they could be moved by the fighters, me following closely behind Luka to protect his back. Our hands rested on the hilts of our weapons. Nevertheless, it did nothing to render the situation any less tense.

A flicker of motion caught the corner of my eye; I grabbed the back of Luka's jacket and yanked. Neither of us were prepared for the result. He wasn't ready to be yanked off balance so, and I wasn't prepared for his weight when he reeled backward and slammed into me. The man that had been thrown, the motion that I had seen, skidded along one of the tables on his front, bowling glasses out of the way so that they shattered on the hard ground on each side of the table. Luka's weight nearly knocked me over; only both of our quick reflexes saved us from falling. My hands snaked around his shoulder to steady him as he grabbed for my arm and twisted so that most of the impact was taken away, ending with us in a tangled embrace. Wolf-whistles rang out through the tavern as our plight momentarily distracted the brawlers. Luka shook his head and stared at the floor, which brought more laughter. I bit my lip tightly and slid around him so that I was in front, dragging him after me as I ploughed through the crowd, to the base of the stairs. A plump woman with the same black hair and tight bun as the much younger barmaid stood in front of us, arms crossed over her ample chest.

I sighed darkly. "May we help you?" I asked, only deigning to choose more polite phrasing when Luka's hand touched my back warningly. The woman reached out to touch me, but dropped her hand when she saw my weapons belt, the silver of the hilts glittering in the soft candlelight. I crossed my arms over my chest and waited, brows arched.

"Are you certain that you want to go upstairs with the likes of him?" she asked, nodding toward Luka. I glanced back at him, at his soft brown hair and even softer blue eyes, his open face with gentle laugh lines and deep dimples fringing full lips.

I couldn't help it; I let out a very unladylike snort. "Believe me, I appreciate the concern, but it is lost on me. I don't need it, and even if I did, if my honor is to be impugned by having someone in a room with me, I'd rather it be him." I jerked my head back at him, smothering a grin at his startled, yet flattered expression. The muscles in his forearm flexed as I dragged him up the stairs after me, swerving to the side and pressing our backs against the wall as the narrow space grew ever more crowded, so much so that we struggled to squeeze by. We were both relatively lean, but there wasn't much room to spare. Giggling women and exceedingly drunk men crowded the hall. At the far end of the hall, I could see our room, the only one that still had the sign on it flipped to "unoccupied." It seemed to be the light at the end of the tunnel.

Luka and I switched places as he used a combination of polite excuses and forceful shoves to clear the way. I grasped the back of his sword belt and watched his back, glaring at anyone who made a move toward us and deflecting a man's hand when he tried to grab my wrist. I had my free hand wrapped tightly around the hilt of my dagger as Luka fumbled with the keys, flipping the sign to "occupied" before we stepped inside. The room was simple but relatively well kept for such a seedy establishment, with a low bed and a tiny night stand. Large, slashing nicks in the wall marked violence from the past. The candles on the nightstand and the desk swam in hard pools of wax, the wicks scorched and burnt. The only chair in the room was canted at an odd angle because one leg was shorter than the others, and by that I meant a large chunk was missing at the bottom, sliced clean through with a sword. We both moved toward the chair, then stopped and swerved toward the bed, once again ending up in each other's way. Luka solved the problem by stepping back, gesturing gallantly for me to choose where I wanted to sit. I chose the bed, while he moved to the chair. He sat and grabbed for the desk as the chair tilted alarmingly. I chuckled quietly.

"Tell me about yourself," he said once we were both settled. I kicked off my boots and tucked my feet under my thighs.

"Is that an order?"

Luca blinked and I rolled my eyes. I was in a strange mood, but it figured that the kind King wouldn't catch the irritation. "Never mind. What do you want to know?"

He tilted his head, the squat, flickering candles casting his lean face in a strange light. I hadn't noticed before the shadow of hair on his sharp chin; he'd been clean shaven when I'd met him but must not have had to time to shave since then. It made him look older, but I was more interested in his eyes, which glittered in the candle light. He caught me looking and raised his brows; I cleared my throat roughly and waited for his response.

"Where did you grow up?"

"In a small town," I responded noncommittally.

"Do you have family?"

I swallowed hard. A phrase had become popular recently, that "time heals all wounds." It isn't true. Bad memories are like stitches. They can be nearly healed, but one mistake, and they are shredded and fresh once again.

"I have not had family in a long time."

"What happened?" he asked gently. He leaned forward, elbows resting on his knees, his face open and comforting as he waited for my answer.

"The plague."

"You lived in a plague village?"

I drew my dagger; Luka stiffened, then relaxed when he realized that I was only twirling it contemplatively around my long fingers, lost in memories. I did feel a flash of either insult or hilarity that he thought I was going to stab him. I didn't think I could have brought myself to do it, even if I'd had to. Certainly not on orders.

"I killed my parents," I murmured painfully, The gems on the hilt of the dagger dug viciously into the healing slash on my palm, but I didn't let go. The pain was less than what I had deserved, I thought, before I exhaled slowly and glanced at Luka, loosening my grip. That way of thinking was the reason for the scars on my wrist, and I refused to let myself be dragged back into that frame of mind.

Luka's face was white as chalk. "What are you talking about?"

"My father was a craftsman, especially with wood and rare stones. When my parents sent me into the next village to deliver one of my father's orders, I didn't know that when I returned, I brought the plague back with me. People started to fall ill; I was the last. I didn't even know how many had died until I woke."

"How many?"

"Twenty three of the plague. Thirty four more of starvation."
Luka froze, the slim light of the candle dancing in his wide
azure eyes as I continued. "The War Queen before this one," I
had to stop myself from calling her by name, "decided to cut her
losses. She ordered the town barricaded and stopped sending
food in. Said she didn't want to waste it on people who wouldn't
survive anyway."

He leaned forward, elbows resting on his knees, his expression avid. "So how then did you survive?" he asked intently.

I sheathed my dagger and leaned back on the bed, loosening
the buckle on my sword belt and removing it, slinging it onto
the bed side table with a sigh of relief for the pinched skin
beneath it. Luka's expression was almost hungry as he watched,
his eyes flicking to catch my motion. I was acutely aware of the
position I was in, bare feet resting on the floor, the hem of my
shirt slid up a tad to reveal the sharp line of my hip. Luka's eyes
rested on the bit of bare skin before he jerked his eyes back up,
twisting the silver ring savagely on his finger. Now was the
perfect moment to ask about it, but the words died in my throat.
I sat up quickly and reached for my boots, shoving my feet back
into them.

"Our meal should be ready pretty soon," I mumbled. "We
may as well head downstairs."

"Wait," Luka said. His voice was husky, his throat flexing as
if it hurt to speak. "What happened? I can't imagine you left
willingly."

I chuckled darkly. "You're right about that. I was fevered
from eating food that was too old. I was unconscious when the
traders came to loot the town."

"That makes more sense. What then?"

I shook my head. "Another time. Let's go." He protested as I
reached the door, but dropped his sword belt and followed me
slowly. I couldn't help but grin as I turned to look at him.

"Kings do not whine," I chided, a parody of what Lana had told me.

"I wasn't born a king," he grumbled, but his lips tilted up. "I can't figure you out. One minute, we're having a perfectly normal, if morbid conversation, and the next you shut down like you've made a terrible mistake. I don't understand you."

"I did make a mistake," I agreed. "And I will be punished for it. The War Queen doesn't like her War Ladies talking about themselves. She thinks it's too easy to use against us, and she may be right." I jabbed him lightly in the chest with one finger, half turning toward the door to put some distance between us. "And you are far too easy to talk to."

Luka's soft voice stopped me in my tracks. "How badly?"

I knew what he meant: my punishment. "Whipped, most likely." My voice sounded different, like it didn't even matter to me. It did, but I had been whipped before. Quite often, actually. Geneva was my friend, but sometimes I wondered if she enjoyed seeing me brought down, put in my place. I was a threat to her throne, after all. If I really chose to, I could bring her down.

"You are very casual about whipping," Luka observed. He hugged himself tightly, his slim fingers tracing the sides of his ribs and onto his back. It was an unconscious movement, one that I understood. Clenching my fists, I could feel the skin on my back stretching tight around the scars. I tugged my shirt up partially; Luka's breath hissed out between his teeth. I twitched as he stroked my scars gently, even though they had stopped hurting long ago.

"Lord in Heaven," he breathed. "How many times have you been flogged?" I counted on my fingers, a habit that had made my tutor livid with rage.

"Insubordination, refusing orders, striking a commanding officer, and treason." I took a breath. "I think that's everything."

Luka's dark brows rose fractionally at the last charge. "It looks like there are more stripes than that," he observed.

I nodded. "More than one time on each charge. Sometimes I took the stripes for others. Better me than them," I said with a grim smile. His features were strained as if he was in pain, but it was only empathy for my own past agony.

We headed downstairs, but this time, I went first. The hallway was even rowdier than before. A couple, and I used the term loosely, was tangled together in front of a closed door; I skirted them carefully. Another woman led a man up the stairs; masculine, drunken snickers followed them up, along with a mug that came flying at their retreating backs, sloshing amber liquid in a wide arc and showering those below. Not that it mattered. They were so drunk they could have bathed in it and the smell wouldn't have been any different. A quick check of the room revealed that Loxxley was still leaning on the bar, chatting animatedly with the barmaid.

Luka and I returned to our table, the only one open. He slid around me, his shoulder brushing mine momentarily, and pulled my chair out for me, ever the gentleman. I smiled and shook my head but thanked him nonetheless, trying to tamp down the feeling that his courtly manners were going to get us mugged. Unfortunately, I happened to be right.

The barmaid promised that our meals would be ready soon, although none of us were in any hurry. I was starving, but I was selfishly glad for a chance to spend more time with Luka without Loxxley, who was leaning on the bar and staring at the barmaid, practically drooling. She was very aware of him; her eyes slid to him every few moments, but neither of them made any move toward each other. I grinned slightly and turned back, only to see Luka tangled in a headlock. He was gasping for breath, his face purple and his eyes wide, but before I could help, he twisted and slammed his sharp elbow into the man's face. Good news: the man fell backward, slamming onto his back on the table behind him, scattering coins and dice in a cloud that clattered to the floor. Bad news: he took Luka with him, bending him backwards and not easing any of the pressure on his throat. Double bad news: the gamblers were not at all happy with having their game interrupted. I jumped forward and tried to drag Luka away from the man who was still holding him, finally resorting to digging my short nails into one of the prominent veins in his captor's wrist rather than continue with this undignified tug of war, with Luka in the middle. The man let out a pained grunt and released Luka, who staggered to his feet and stood at my side, grabbing my shoulder for support. Breath rasping in his throat, he gasped quietly, bent over and rubbing his throat with the hand not braced on my shoulder. I put my hand over the one on my shoulder, giving it a warning squeeze when the men at the messy table rose slowly, ominously.

In the struggle, nearly all of the coins had ended up on the floor in a sprawl of gold, silver, and copper. The dice were down there as well, not to mention the mugs of ale that the men had been sipping from, probably all night. The one cup that wasn't on the floor was clenched in the leader's white knuckled fist, but the contents had sloshed down his front, a dark stain on his grimy shirt and short pants. Instinctively, I reached for my sword, but Luka and I had both left our weapons belts in the room, deciding that it would be best if two clearly aristocratic men and an armed woman didn't show up armed to the teeth. I was regretting that decision now. Judging by the grim smile on Luka's mouth, he was as well. He straightened up, still rubbing his throat and sparing only a glance for the man who had grabbed him, presumably to steal the coin purse that dangled from his belt. The man was clutching his wrist with very unmasculine tears in his eyes, and I swallowed a startled grin. Apparently I had done more damage than I had intended, but I couldn't bring myself to be sorry if it had saved Luka, who couldn't stop rubbing his throat. While he seemed steady on his feet at the moment, I had a bad feeling that wouldn't hold true.

"Excuse us for interrupting your game, gentleman," Luka said politely, his courtly manners once again making an appearance, despite the rasp of his voice and the pained face he made when he had to speak. I wrinkled my nose at the word "gentleman," a description that fit these goons about as well as calling the little donkey tethered in the courtyard a warhorse. It was embarrassing on all counts. The men didn't seem to be swayed by his manners, however. Their eyes were red and shot with blood, although whether that was from anger or drink I couldn't have said. I shifted so that I was slightly in front of Luka, but he stepped up to my side, meeting my glare levelly. I glanced around for Loxxley, ready to leave the situation before it escalated, and almost missed the punch that came flying at my face.

I ducked instinctively, dropping to the floor and kicking my booted foot at the goons' ankles with all my might. They collapsed like pins, but one managed to grab Luka on his way down, once again starting the tug of war over Luka. A hand wrapped around my ankle and I kicked out, wondering briefly why we always had to get into fights.

It wouldn't do to reenter camp with bruises and, I thought painfully, a broken rib, but that seemed to be how it would work out. Luka and I picked our way out of the remains of the gambling table and the gamblers themselves, under Loxxley's cool stare. He had not come to our aid in the massive fight, the one that had left six drunkards unconscious on the floor, several tables smashed, and the two of us limping painfully. The innkeeper just sighed deeply and continued to clean a mug with a once white rag. The dark haired woman who had warned me away from Luka earlier, whom I thought might be the innkeeper's wife, grabbed a broom rather aggressively and swept out from behind the counter, skirts swishing. She set to work, stepping none too gently on each of the fallen drunks and sweeping shattered glass and pottery into a neat pile, with another for the dice and other gambling paraphernalia. The other girl came out from behind the bar as well; Luka helped her to right all the tipped tables and chairs, as well as the stools from the bar that had somehow ended up all the way across the room. I could vaguely remember one being hurled at my face, but that only accounted for one. I was uncertain of the others.

Luka touched my shoulder lightly and retreated to the fire, where there were a few mismatched chairs. I lowered myself into one, balancing one hand on the arm with the other tucked tightly to my stomach. Judging by the crunch I had heard when punching, most certainly not the man's nose, at least one bone in my hand was broken. To distract myself until we could go upstairs and clean up, I glanced at Luka.

He seemed exhausted, long hair sliding into his face as his head hung, but he looked up, almost as if he could sense my stare. His full lower lip was deeply split, probably from hitting his teeth, just like mine was. A bruise blackened the skin around his eye, and a tiny cut spanned the bridge of his nose. Luka's head was drooping once again, so I followed his lead and leaned my head back against the soft material of the chair, cradling my injured hand against my stomach and propping my cheek on the other. I could hear the ongoing cleanup through a haze of exhaustion, but I didn't move. Soon enough I had dropped off to sleep.

I awoke to a dull throbbing in my temples. My eyes still closed, I held perfectly still, forcing my muscles to stay loose when gentle hands touched me. I was still in the chair where I had fallen asleep. I had no weapons, but then, I hadn't had any when I had fallen asleep. I could hear soft voices, and I strained to hear them, my eyelids straining with the effort not to open them.

"Leave her be. She's not bothering anyone where she is, and she's getting much needed sleep. You of all people should know that the injured need more rest than the rest of us."

The voice was too deep to be Luka's, which meant it was Loxxley. He seemed to be advocating to leave me be, something I appreciated, but I didn't understand that last bit. I could feel the skin between my eyebrows twitch as I fought not to raise them, but I hoped that it could pass for a motion made in sleep.

"I would greatly appreciate it if you didn't throw my illness in my face like that, brother." There was an edge to Luka's normally calm voice that I hadn't heard before. "Besides, she'll regret falling asleep here in the morning. She's helped us more than either of us would care to admit. With any luck, we'll reach her queen on the morrow, and seeing as she is likely to be the only one in the entire camp that might intervene on our behalf, it makes sense to ensure that she is in top form. That won't happen if she sleeps down here."

"Leave her be," Loxxley insisted. "We'll care for her hand in the morning and be on our way." I was actually relatively comfortable here, and trying to share a room with one bed and one rickety chair amongst three people wouldn't be comfortable in the slightest, so I nestled deeper in the chair and listened to the boys scurry away. I drifted back into sleep with a smile on my face.

Chapter Twelve

By some miracle, I managed to sneak into the room, retrieve my clothes, and slip back out with neither Luka nor Loxxley, sleeping soundly, any the wiser. Luka was sprawled on the bed, black and blue hands folded over his flat stomach. The water in the the basin was tinged with pink, a bloody rag draped over the edge. A half unspooled roll of bandages sat next to it, along with a knife and a needle, both too clean to have been put to use. The window was open, so I padded across and closed it carefully, rolling my eyes. These two would catch their death not on the blade of a sword, but from the cold breeze of a window being open all night.

Once downstairs a safe distance from the boys, I tugged my boots on and snuck out the back door into the stable courtyard, slipping into an empty stall and hurriedly changing clothes. Despite the early hour, the horses were awake. A solid, consistent thump made me smile. Sin stretched her neck out over the half door as far as it could go, the silky black mane rippling in the rising sun. I lengthened my strides and gave her thick neck a solid pat, passing the grooms on their rounds. None of them paid me any mind, too busy with their early morning chores to be concerned with a stranger in their midst. I followed one of them to the grain bin and searched the room until I found a wooden bucket to fill. Returning to Sin's stall with the full bucket, I hung it on a peg and found a box of brushes, then set to work. She stuck her dark nose in the full bucket, snuffling and crunching loudly. I glanced at her and made a face, but couldn't help the smile that tugged at my lips.

"Your manners are atrocious. Have I not taught you better?"

She snorted and flattened her ears, taking a half hearted swipe at me with her blunt teeth. I swiped back with the brush and we went on like that for a few moments, chasing each other around within the confines of the stall. I flattened myself against the wall and dropped the brush, holding my hands up in surrender as I panted softly; I was already tired, and I needed to be fresh for the long day ahead in case anything happened. If Sin needed to think that she had bested me, then so be it. Finally, satisfied that she had me on the run, Sin shook her thick black mane triumphantly and went back to her oats. I gave her one last stroke with the soft bristles of the brush and stepped out.

Something scuffed on the stones behind me and I whirled, drawing a short dagger from a sheath on my wrist. The boy held his hands up in surrender, nearly dropping the mug that he was carrying. His wide, terrified eyes dropped as soon as I had sheathed it; I took the mug from him with a nod of thanks.

"I meant nothing by it, my lady," he murmured. "Your..." he hesitated, clearly unsure what to call Luka and Loxxley, and I motioned for him to continue, trying to save us both some time. No matter what he said, no doubt he would be afraid of offending me, and I honestly wasn't sure what to call them. The closest would perhaps be "charges", but even that would only apply to Luka, since Loxxley was more like an unwelcome hanger-on. Perhaps "nuisances" would be more appropriate. "The men are waiting for you inside."

I thanked him, checked on Sin once more, then headed back into the inn. My wrist itched, and I shifted the sheath to make it more comfortable, short dagger rattling. It was the only weapon on me at the moment, but when I was the one wielding it, it should be more than enough for any opponent I might face. This close to home, I could feel my strength returning. Or perhaps it was that I was finally beginning to heal. The tattoo on my shoulder was no longer a constant pain, which had meant that either I was in constant danger the entire time I was retrieving Luka, or that the magic had been on the fritz; I was inclined to believe it was the latter. Now it was only a low tingle, like it understood that we were close to home. Perhaps it did.

I raised my fist to knock on the door, a quick skip of knuckles on hardwood. The response was almost immediate, accompanied by shuffling on the other side and a muffled oath before the door opened, revealing two very rumpled and very tired men. Loxxley's hair was damp, swept sideways on his forehead; there was a suspicious red mark on the side of his neck. I swallowed a comment but couldn't hide a grin. Luka's eyes were glazed with sleep, his hair rumpled and his body slumped, but he perked up when I mentioned food, as did Loxxley. They both ducked back into the room to grab sword belts, then thought better of it when they noticed that mine was missing. I felt naked without it, since it was usually the first thing I put on in the morning after my clothes, but I figured it would be better for everyone if the three of us didn't seem to pose any immediate danger to the other patrons, given the events of last night.

I led the way down the hallway, Luka hot on my heels and Loxxley bringing up the rear. The common room was mostly empty, with only a few yawning travelers downing a strong brown liquid and a drunk or two nursing their hangovers, hands clamped around their temples as if to hold the pounding in or the noise of the tavern out. I felt a brief twinge of sympathy; I knew how that felt. Nevertheless, we had places to be and little time to get there, so I headed for the bar, only to swerve away when I saw that Loxxley was already ordering a morning meal. I could only hope this sudden spurt of manners extended for the rest of the journey. Luka was already seated, resting his cheek on his hand only to jerk his head back up when his hand touched a bruise, though whether it was the black and blue one ringing his eye or one of many on his hand, splayed across his knuckles, I couldn't tell. There were more small cuts on his face than I had noticed last night.

I joined him, lowering myself carefully into the chair as I had last night, with one hand on the armrest and my injured hand tucked tightly to my stomach. I stretched it out on the table, since the throbbing pain eased a bit when it wasn't bent. Luka roused himself from his stupor and reached shyly across the table, touching my outstretched fingers gently. I didn't move, although a tiny voice at the back of my mind insisted I heed the silver ring on his hand. He must have noticed me looking, for he flushed and twisted it self-consciously around his slender finger.

"Before I was crowned, I promised myself that I would change things. No more arranged marriages, or class distinctions that kept couples apart. That I would make the warrior arts accessible to anyone; you of all people know that a woman can fight as well as a man, or better. But sometimes necessity forces us to do things that we never thought we would do."

My stomach dropped, and I swallowed slowly. An arranged marriage I could understand. I myself was the product of an arranged marriage, although that was more because my mother's prospects had been so limited. In our country, young women were as encouraged to be warriors as they were to be mothers, but my mother had been born with a physical deformity, a twisted right leg, which prevented her from doing anything remotely physical. To be frank, not only did I not know where I had gotten my fighting tendencies from, I also didn't know how she had had me in the first place. However, she had, and had raised me well for the first decade of my life, when she had died of a sudden infection. After her death, my father had remarried. Although my stepmother was young and gentle, she never tried to prevent me from playing with swords and blunt knives, which was as far as I had gotten with weapons training before the plague. However, I had been as saddened by her death as with that of my real mother, and I was grateful to this day that she had never stopped my learning.

"Who is she?" I asked, trying to sound like I didn't care what the answer was, when in fact I really did. I so rarely found a man, or woman for that matter, that I cared to pursue romantically; it was just my luck that he was promised to someone else.

He was still twisting the ring on his finger, a blush creeping up his throat. "A lady whose father helped us when there was little food to be had. I suppose I should be lucky that she even agreed, given my..."

"Illness," I finished. He looked puzzled, so I explained. "I was partially awake last night when Loxxley mentioned it. I didn't mean to overhear." I vaguely remembered the economic downturn that must have prompted his betrothal. It had been several years ago, when the torrential rains had flooded every inch of farmland in several countries, completely destroying the crops. Geneva had dug deeply into the royal reserves to buy food for her subjects; I had done some things that I wasn't proud of in order to get that food to where it was needed most. While I wasn't necessarily proud of it, I didn't regret any of it either. That must have been at the very beginning of Luka's reign as War King. I wasn't surprised that he had had to make a deal to help his people; I was both impressed at his dedication and saddened that it had come to that. I wasn't sure that I would have been able to make such a difficult decision.

"I didn't want you to find out like that," Luka mumbled. "I wanted to tell you myself. Before we reached your queen, but there just hasn't been time." He took a deep breath. "It's not constant. Most of the time, I am fine, and you can not even tell that I am sick. Occasionally, however, my body locks up, and I can not seem to move. Loxxley is always with me, to watch over me, in case it happens while I'm fighting."

"And you're afraid it will." I could see in his eyes that he was terrified this weakness would descend on him in the midst of a battle, that he would die because of something he could not control. I wanted to comfort him, could feel the need to shiver through me so hard that my tattoo flared, but I couldn't. No doubt today would be the last that I would see of him. If Geneva ever found out about my feelings for him, whatever they may be, there would be hell to pay. Not only that, but I could imagine what the other ladies would think, their pitying looks at the fact that I thought that I was good enough for a king. I tightened my fists, short nails carving marks into both palms, shattering pain driving through my injured hand.

I could see Loxxley making his way back to the table, finally, helping the barmaid that he had no doubt spent the night with to carry trays loaded with full plates to break our fast. I had seen him in the room in the morning, but I hadn't seen him last night. Not that it mattered. Where he had spent the night was none of my concern. I groped for any topic to turn our dour conversation into something that Loxxley wouldn't comment on; I didn't think I could handle what he would think of the current discussion.

"What about your dog?" I blurted, much more loudly than I had intended, cringing inwardly. "Rupert, wasn't it?" Loxxley's brows arched toward his hairline as he seated himself; Luka looked positively bewildered, but he answered gamely.

"There are people looking after him while I'm gone." Inwardly, I panicked. Of course someone would be taking care of his dog. The lowliest peasant could find someone to take care of their hound. It was the charm of dogs. He was a King with a fleet of servants; he probably could have ordered them all to wait on his dog hand and paw and the running of the palace would never suffer. Why had I chosen this as the topic of conversation? Surely I was clever enough to come up with something else.

Luka was still staring intently at me in puzzlement, but Loxxley diverted his attention, for which I was grateful. I shoveled food onto my plate from the platter in the center of the table. Thickly sliced ham oozed juice on a sturdy platter; a pile of fluffy biscuits overshadowed a small bowl of melted butter, with a blunt knife across the mouth of the bowl. The barmaid from last night came to our table with a tray filled with mugs of some sort of sparkling amber liquid that bubbled on my tongue with my first experimental sip. The barmaid laughed at my expression and tilted the pitcher over the mug to refill it, her full lips turned up. There was a red mark on her neck that was a near perfect match to the one on Loxxley's; Luka and I shared a knowing glance before I remembered myself and my gaze skittered away.

"Have you never had apple cider, my lady?"

I shook my head and took another careful sip, enjoying the bubbles on my tongue. "No, I haven't, because up until now, I had no idea that such a thing even existed. Rest assured, I will inquire about it from now on. Thank you." It was the best thing that I had ever tasted. If we didn't have this in my kingdom, we were about to discover it, and if we did I wanted to know why no one had ever informed me of its existence before. It was a severe oversight.

Once I had finished eating and slurping down the remainder of my apple cider, I excused myself to the stables. With my emotions so in turmoil, I didn't think I could handle Luka riding with me even for the last day; the only thing worse was how badly the brothers would be at one another's throats if they had to ride double on Loxxley's stallion, who had been doing perfectly well so far. It would be a shame to ruin everyone's day, including the horses'. On that note, the first order of business while the boys were finishing their meal was to find Luka a horse, one that would be able to keep up with Sin and Loxxley's fine mount until we reached Geneva, hopefully by this evening or early on the morrow. I flagged down one of the grooms, who pointed me to the horsemaster, who told me that a party had left a gelding here nearly a week ago due to an injury to one of his front legs and had taken another in his place. The injury was healed, and so the horsemaster informed me that he would be fine for travel.

I thanked him and sought out the gelding. He was far older than either Sin or the stallion, his dark head gray at the muzzle with prominent whiskers that twitched when he whinnied welcomingly. I stroked his head gently and slid a rope over his head, looping it behind his ears and over his nose. He looked perfectly acceptable to me, if not up to the standards that we were used to for our mounts, but a big part of whether or not he would be coming with us depended on if he got along with the others. I led him down the row to where Loxxley's white stallion was stabled, my grip on the rope tight just in case he was as ill tempered with the old fellow as he had been with Sin. However, the white gave a friendly nudge and went back to his oats. I could only hope that it went as well with Sin, but I tied the gelding in the courtyard and led Sin out to meet him. It would be easier to gauge her reaction to him when it was a neutral place, not in her stall, where she was confined and therefore much more likely to lash out at anything or anyone but me. Her dark head lowered and she swung her hindquarters nervously, bumping my back and shoving me forward a step. With her ears pinned and her head thrown up high, neck arched, she was giving all the indications of not wanting to be friendly today, so I tried to pull her back, only to have her yank the rope out of my hands and stop in front of the gelding. I started to move forward, then froze for fear of ruining the moment. Her nostrils flared as she sniffed him, then acquiesced and touched noses gently. With that settled, I took them both by their ropes and set about readying to head out.

"So this fellow is mine, I take it?" Luka's voice startled me where I crouched to check Sin's hoof for a stone. I jerked upright, cracking my head onto the hitching post in the court-yard and dropping Sin's heavy hoof roughly onto the cobbles in the process. Rubbing my head as I stood, I nodded curtly at Luka and swung into the saddle, slightly less gracefully than usual because Sin stepped forward mid-swing. I gathered up the reins and tried not to notice Luka's hurt expression, which he wrenched back to nothing in moments. Loxxley was still tight-ening the buckles of his saddle bags, checking to ensure that they were securely fastened to the saddle; he motioned for Luka to go ahead. I started to follow Luka, but Loxxley yanked the reins, the white stallion's hooves clattering as he jerked into Sin's path. Sin threw her head up with a protesting whinny and rose half into a rear; I shoved her down, my hands fisted in the thick mane at the top of her neck, and glared at Loxxley.

"And just what do you think you're doing?" I hissed viciously. We were the same height, so we were eye to eye over the plunging horses. It was a struggle to keep Sin from going after the stallion, and while I was thoroughly angry with his rider, he couldn't be held accountable for that. If Sin had decided to take a swipe at Loxxley, it might have been a different story.

"I know how you feel about my brother. I'm telling you nothing good can come of it, so let it go. Once we reach your queen, you'll never see him again. Accept that. It's better for everyone."

There was a nearly audible hiss as my seething anger was cooled by the fact that he was right, like a red hot horseshoe steeped in a bucket of water. When I answered, it was with difficulty. "I don't know what you're talking about." We both knew that it was a lie, but I had to at least try. Even if he didn't believe me, I had at least kept up appearances.

Loxxley shook his head grimly, finally pulling his horse aside so that we could follow Luka, who waited at the edge of the courtyard, his expression concerned. He didn't interfere, not that it would have changed anything.

Chapter Thirteen

"Not that way," I called. Luka glanced back, his dark brows drawn together in confusion.

"Because the quickest way to draw attention is to ride through the capital city with a War Lady. Everyone in the city will know you are here in minutes."

"That's what I'm here for." I whipped around in my saddle so fast that my lower back cracked. Reaga smiled wanly and flexed her fingers gently in a sort of wave. I straightened up in my saddle and reached out, motioning for her to turn her head. She did so slowly, revealing a jagged slash that ripped up her face, from the corner of her jaw and into her hairline. I bit down a gasp and nodded slowly, taking in the entirety of her appearance with more care. Her dark faced bay mare was absent; instead she was seated on a much larger red roan, one that dwarfed her. All around, she seemed much smaller than usual, her slender shoulders bowed forward. Pain was written across her face and seemed to pour down her body. Luka and Loxxley just stared, like they couldn't figure out what she was doing here, so I urged Sin to the side; Reaga did the same, stopping the roan next to Luka.

"You will be going with Reaga to the castle. No one would expect you not to be with me, so if you go the back way with her, no one would even consider that you are anyone of import," I explained, still refusing to make eye contact. Out of the corner of my eye, I could see him shifting in the saddle, but I resolutely looked away. Reaga was explaining their route to the castle while Loxxley and I started slowly working through the crowd to the main entrance; I could feel Luka's gaze boring into my back, but I refused to look back.

The city was beautiful, if I did say so myself. The gray cobbled streets were swept each night so as to be clean in the morning. It was mid morning already, the sun working its way up into the sky to beat down on our heads, so the streets were no longer spotless. The castle rose high and majestic at the far end of the city, behind huge, polished marble walls. The massive stained glass windows shone in the sun. On either side of the immense bridge that marked the entrance to the city, boats with sleek sails raised to the sky slipped into their places at the docks. An intricate system of water wheels, the largest at the center with smaller ones radiating out like the rays of a sunburst, was one of several sources of energy for the capital city. Every one of the bridges could be raised or lowered with a set of massive wheels tucked safely in the gate house. Bridges of various sizes acted as a multi-level avenue for travel; the tactical idea behind it was that if one part of the city was compromised, the bridges to the others could be raised, preventing any attackers from reaching other areas or escaping. Arches rose above each bridge, painted intricately with the name. The largest, directly in the center of the city, had a clock that could be seen from anywhere in the city. Despite the marvels of the city, nothing could compare to the castle itself.

Loxxley must have come to the same conclusion, whistling softly under his breath. "Beautiful. But I prefer ours."

"One almost always prefers their own home over another's," I pointed out, then bit my lip when I thought about what I had said. I didn't know what Loxxley and Luka's early home life had been like, but my home was now a burnt out shell of its former self, no longer inhabitable by anything larger than a fox. The same could be said for the rest of my village. However, this was my home now, had been for the past years, and I was duly proud of it. I hadn't had any part in building it, but the taxes that I paid from my commission did play a part in keeping it at its finest.

"Reaga will take Luka the long way to the castle, likely to the servants' entrance at the rear. We will take the main paths, making sure to move as normally as possible. People will expect the person of import to be with me, so if they see us together, most won't even bat an eye."

Loxxley removed one gloved hand from the reins and held it over his heart, feigning hurt. "Are you saying that I'm not important?"

"Yes," I said flatly, too tired and sick of the deceptions to be polite. Almost immediately I felt bad for my bluntness. My home was so close that I could feel it in bones, and the low ache in my shoulder finally eased. I would see to it that Loxxley and his brother were safely delivered to Geneva, and my responsibilities ended there. Once that was done, I would go on my way, and probably never see either of them again. The thought made my heart pang, but I pushed it down and set my eyes on the castle. I told myself that it wouldn't do to get distracted now, but somewhere deep down, I wondered if perhaps my heart wished the opposite.

Sin's ears, low and floppy with ease as we picked our way through the city, pricked straight up. My tattoo gave a warning throb and I jerked up straight in the saddle, reaching for my sword, which hung from my saddle with the sheathed blade brushing Sin's shoulder and the gleaming silver hilt within easy reach. The road ahead was blocked by a milling crowd, which almost never happened here on the main road. War Ladies were never more than a few minutes away in the castle, so most disagreements or other issues were resolved before we ever arrived. However, this time, that didn't seem to be the case. The crowd was rowdy, pushing and shoving to get a better look at whomever or whatever was in the center of the throng. My tattoo was still pounding, and I drew my sword without hesitation. Sin pushed her way through the crowd with her chest; I held my sword out to the side and the crowd scrambled back. The source of the ruckus was two men, squaring off in the middle of a wide circle, staggering drunkenly and waving dull swords at one another. I sighed darkly and swung my right leg over the front of my saddle, boot heel swishing over Sin's mane. Before I could dismount fully, Loxxley drew his own sword and dropped down, motioning for me to stay where I was.

"I can handle this, if you'll give me a moment." He paused to wait for my permission. I was surprised at the sudden courtesy, especially after I had just insulted him. I would have to apologize sooner rather than later but in the meantime, there was work to be done.

I waved for him to do what he was going to, sheathing my sword and leaning back in the saddle with my arms crossed over my chest as I waited for him to finish. I contemplated whether to sit properly and finally decided to swing my leg back over; on the off chance that he needed my help, it wouldn't take long for me to dismount. He waded through the crowd, sword drawn, and stopped when he got close to the men. His lips moved, but he was angled away from me in such a way that I could not make out what he was saying. The men wavered, gesturing and shouting emphatically. I still couldn't make out what was being said, but when Loxxley reached into his belt purse and dropped a few gold coins into each man's hand, that spoke clearly enough. The men dipped their heads at one another and thanked Loxxley, which was obvious enough with their deep bows and practically toothless grins. Loxxley strode back to his horse as the crowd dispersed, white teeth flashing in a smug smile.

"Did you have any doubts?"

I rolled my eyes and picked up the reins, refusing to dignify that with a response. The smile stayed on his lips, but mine dropped as I stared ahead. From the entrance to the city, all had seemed well. Instead, as we rode closer to the castle, I realized that everything was not as it seemed. As with all cities, parts of it were better kept than others. When I had left there had been soldiers patrolling the city with a few posted at the entrances to the seedier parts of the city; that was still the same, but what was different was that the entrances had been blocked off, tall gates with massive locks cutting off any way in, or out, of the areas. I swung in my saddle and could see that the locked gates were now common, visible at every corner of the square. Many of the buildings, in such good condition before, were on a decline, the bricks crumbling or charred. The kitchens where food was provided for the poor were closed; there were no beggars to be seen, which was strange.

As soon as I thought it, however, a woman's hand touched my knee. I jerked and Loxxley lunged for the blade at his wrist, but I shook my head and leaned down to better hear the tiny woman. I knew her, not personally, but I had seen her a few times and dropped coins into her basket on my way out of the city, like I did for most of the less fortunate. Her graying hair was cropped short. The hand on my knee was thin and veined with blue, but her grip was tight, filthy nails digging into the tender points on the sides of my leg. I winced again as she stretched up onto her toes, but it was clear that, between my height and Sin's, she was never going to be tall enough to be in the same vicinity. I swung my leg over the saddle and jumped down.

"Lady Tara." Her voice was breathy. "Your man is in trouble."

I glanced up at Loxxley. He arched a brow, not even bothering to hide the fact that he was listening to our conversation, but the woman's hand tugged more insistently. "Not him. The other one. His brother."

Loxxley stiffened. "What makes you think that we are brothers?"

"Your looks. You have the same look." I frowned in confusion. In facial features, they did have the same look, but not in hair or eye color; it struck me as odd that someone on the street had looked closely enough at the two of them to see that they were brothers. The woman was clearly in no mood for my hesitation. She waved her hand impatiently and tried to crawl onto Sin's back, who swung her head and flicked her ears, puzzled by this skinny creature attempting to climb her the same way one would a wall. I stopped myself before I helped her.

"Before we go any further, what do you mean when you say that he's in trouble?"

She glanced around to see if anyone else was listening, but other than Loxxley, no one else was paying any attention. People on the street tended not to pay attention to beggars; they would rather avoid them at all costs. Anyone who had lived in the city for long knew that the War Ladies appreciated their privacy. They didn't look or interact with us unless they were asked. "The Queen is... not herself. Hasn't been for quite some time, but there's no hiding it now. I've a friend that's a servant in the castle, and she told me that someone is whispering in the

Queen's ear, convincing her that your boy is a spy. She is putting on some sort of ball tomorrow evening, to prove her suspicions. To show all her nobles what happens to those who dare plot against her."

"If he were going to send a spy, he certainly wouldn't risk coming here himself," I pointed out. My mind whirled. A ball, with everyone who was anyone invited, would put all of us in danger, especially if Geneva viewed us all as her enemies. The woman's tiny hands disappeared into the folds of her skirt, twisting the dingy fabric anxiously.

"I see the sense, but the Queen hasn't seen sense in a long time." She cringed slightly as my hands tightened reflexively on the reins; she must have thought that I was going to hit her, which couldn't be further from the truth. If anything, I wanted to hit myself. If what this woman said was true, then I was at fault for anything that happened here. Especially to Luka. I had been gone a lot recently, but that didn't excuse my failure to notice something so huge. I should have noticed Geneva's behavior and put a stop to it long ago. If I had, then Luka wouldn't be in danger.

Loxxley's stallion sidled a step and I snapped out of my reverie as his shoulder bumped mine. I was responsible for past failures, and it was my job to fix them. I looked at the little woman and then at Loxxley, who raised his brows expectantly.

"We have much to do. We have a ball to attend."

Chapter Fourteen

"Where are we going?"

I rolled my eyes. That had to be at least the fourth time he had asked me that in that past ten minutes, and I had already answered his question multiple times. "I told you. We are going to my home. We will be safe to prepare for the ball there."

"I thought all War Ladies lived in the castle, so that you are always close to the Queen."

"I said my home, not where I live."

"That clears that right up." There was a frustrated grunt and a jingle of tack behind me. Curious as to what Loxxley had done, I twisted in my saddle. His head was in his hands, his broad shoulders bowed forward; the jingle of tack had been him dropping his reins. He was steering with his knees, not that his horse needed any instruction. The white stallion plodded along, his head bobbing. I couldn't help a snort of laughter as I turned around. We were only around the corner from my home, which was on the edge of the city, near one of the smaller, lesser used gates. I hadn't heard Loxxley pick his reins back up, which probably meant that he wasn't looking. He wouldn't see my home until after we had already stopped, which was fine with me.

"Loxxley, look up." He didn't listen, so I reached out and tapped the white stallion's wither. It was a gentle tap, but he spooked sideways nevertheless, forcing Loxxley to take his head out of his hands in order to soothe him. "What is this place?"

I swung my leg over the front of my saddle and stepped down. Loxxley did the same; I could feel his eyes boring into my back as I rushed to embrace the two women who stood there waiting for me. The dark haired one first, who squeezed my shoulder gently, experimentally. I fought down a wince but couldn't help reaching up to touch it gently. The other woman, more sedate, kissed my cheek gently.

"I'm so sorry about Eili. I knew you two were close." I squeezed my eyes shut and breathed carefully. The pain of losing Eili had been dulled by the journey, and by my fervent attempts not to remember it. Even when we had returned to the city, the last place where all of the War Ladies had been together, I had still been so focused on delivering Luka and Loxxley safely to Geneva that I had been able to keep the pain at bay. Now, with this news about Geneva, all the pain came flooding back. Along with the pain came a deep sense of failure. I had failed to find Eili's killer; I hadn't even begun the hunt. Now, to find out that Geneva had some sort of mysterious illness, that she had been degrading in front of my eyes and that I had never even noticed, drove home the point that I wasn't the invincible warrior everyone believed me to be. I had already known that, but now it was painfully apparent.

"Thank you," I said gently. She nodded.

"Dinner will be ready soon," Vita promised. Her dark hair swayed over her shoulders as she retreated into the house. Kinnia hesitated a moment longer, then unlocked the door to the stable for me and slipped into the house. Loxxley followed me into the stable. There were three stalls, each separated by a thick wooden wall, with a bar in the front. I dropped Sin's reins and lifted the bars from the fronts of two of the stalls. Loxxley was already removing the white stallion's saddle, but when I looked up, he was staring at me.

"What?"

"Who is Eili? Your servant said that you were close with her, but you've not mentioned her, or anyone else for that matter. I know you talked to my brother when you shared the room with him, but he didn't mention you referring to anyone named Eili."

I swallowed hard. "She was another War Lady. She died recently, just before I came to bring your brother here. And what a mistake that has turned out to be," I muttered grimly. I wondered if it might help to talk about Eili's death, and of the two brothers, Loxxley was the one that I would have preferred to tell. Luka would have listened and been his gentle soul, likely touching my arm and saying something to comfort me, but I didn't want that. I wanted someone to listen and move on; I was sure that Loxxley could and would do that for me, so I took a deep breath and spoke softly. "We were escorting a group of young ladies and some of them were giving Eili fits. I sent her to the front of the caravan to scout. We were ambushed. Eili was the only one to die, but that was when I was injured." I reached up to touch my shoulder and bowed my head. I took a deep breath and glanced up at Loxxley to see his reaction.

Loxxley was pale, made even paler by his thick blond hair. "I'm sorry about your friend," was all he said. I nodded my acceptance, and we stayed quiet as we cared for our mounts. For the first time since we had met, my tattoo no longer throbbed in his presence. It had settled from a dull ache to nothingness, allowing the silence to be comfortable.

Dinner was a large meat pie, with mashed potatoes and a

bowl of fruits. Loxxley was a perfect gentleman, which was a surprise. At every inn and waystation we had stopped at on our journey, we hadn't had to worry about fitting three people into one room, because Loxxley had always spent the night elsewhere, with a companion. I watched him carefully, but he said or did nothing untoward around my girls. He handed the bowls around the table, careful to keep his long fingers to himself. The two older ladies watched him shrewdly; I noticed they had arranged the seating so that he was as far away from my third girl, a girl about my age named Marian, who would be most likely to be affected by his charms. Or rather by his looks, as she didn't speak and couldn't hear anyone else speak either. Her skin was flushed, but she refused to look at him through the entirety of the meal, and excused herself as soon as she was finished to make an appointment with my tailor. The others cleaned up the table and slipped out, leaving Loxxley and me to strategize. We would be ready for anything that happened tomorrow. We had to be.

Chapter Fifteen

Riding a horse in a dress is hard. Even if I had been inclined to ride saddle seat, which I wasn't, leather on bare skin pinches uncomfortably. Riding astride, you also have the added detriment of it being breezy in certain areas. I urged Sin into line with the other War Ladies, through the crowd of cheering citizens. Every time a ball or other function of state took place at the castle, we paraded through the city, shaking hands and waving at the crowds of people who were pretending that they weren't terrified of or seeking something from us. This time, there was an extra, one who got more than his fair share of strange looks. Loxxley rode at my side on his white stallion, both of them proud and strong. We were all dressed in our finery, and despite whatever strange feelings I may or may not have been harboring for his brother, even I couldn't deny how good he looked. His thick blond hair glowed in the setting sun. Dressed all in black, his cloak was a verdant forest green, with gold braid at the neck. The same golden thread wound around his throat and cuffs. Hidden beneath his cloak, his family crest was sewn in gold in the center of his back, between his shoulder blades. I had tried to convince him not to wear such an obvious symbol of his allegiance to the ball, as it would put him in danger if Geneva truly thought Luka was a spy and had him thrown into the dungeons. However, he was confident that no one in my country would know enough about the houses from another country to know the difference. I couldn't shake a lingering feeling of unease, not lessened by the fiery prickling of my tattoo.

The ride through the city was uneventful; all too soon, the drawbridge of Geneva's castle loomed above us, creaking on its chains as it was lowered. Hooves clicking on the hardwood, we cantered into the courtyard. With an almost eerie groan, the gate rose behind us and slammed into place. Loxxley swung down from the saddle and hurried around Sin's head to give me a hand down. For the first time since I had met him, he wasn't wearing any weapons, not his sword, or even a dagger. Only War Ladies and friends of the Queen were permitted to wear weapons at official functions within the castle. Loxxley certainly didn't fit either of those descriptions, so our only weapons in a pinch would be mine. I had planned accordingly. If it turned out that Geneva had taken Luka captive, I wasn't sure that I would currently qualify as a friend of the Queen either, but one of two, being a War Lady, would have to do.

Whatever else dresses are, if you know what you are doing, they are a treasure trove of places to hide weapons. My dress was midnight blue, with the collar rising to my neck and the neckline a neat square across my chest. It was intentionally designed to hide my shoulder, and the tattoo there. Nearly all of the other War Ladies had completely bare shoulders, skin flashing in the torchlight as we passed each bracket, but my tailor had been more creative when designing my outfit. It showed enough skin not to be dowdy, in the form of a slit halfway up my right thigh. The long, billowy sleeves hid as many daggers as I could fit, which was quite a few. I had taken my duty to outfit us both with weapons very seriously. I could only hope that the old woman was wrong, that we wouldn't need them. I hadn't spoken to Reaga since last night, but I hoped that Luka was safe in the castle and not already in the dungeons.

The sound of music floated down the hall long before we reached the open doors of the ballroom. A man's voice soared smooth and clear, accompanied by several stringed instruments. I knew that voice, and couldn't help the smile on my face. Ellis nodded as we entered the room, his song never faltering, but my smile dropped as I noticed that his was absent. Any doubt about if what the old woman had said was true vanished. Ellis always had a smile, but now he looked quietly in pain, like he was trying to send a message with his eyes. I searched for Luka with a rising sense of alarm that abated only slightly when I saw him, seated at the high table with Geneva and the other nobles, which puzzled me. The point of bringing him here in disguise had been to keep his identity a secret, and yet there he was, seated with all the other important members of state. Something was very, very wrong here. My tattoo was pounding painfully, so hard it made my head thump. I slid a dagger from my sleeve and passed it to Loxxley. Something was odd about Luka being seated at the high table, and I was going to find out what.

"Take this and stay here," I murmured to Loxxley, using the noise of the gathering to cover my speech. I slipped the crowd as quietly as I could, smiling and nodding to anyone who addressed me but doing my best not to stop. The marble floor was crowded, so I was forced to hug the wall, skirting braziers, guards, and servers with trays of wine or small bits of food as I headed toward the head table. They were deep in conversation, so no one noticed my approach, around the back of the table, against the wall. No one but Luka. His chin tilted down and to the side, tracking my motion over his shoulder.

I crept closer to the table. Luka wasn't seated at the main table, as I had thought; it was a trick of the way that he and the table were placed. His chair was farther back, away from the others by a few feet. I could also see why he was so strangely still. Thin, strong chains shackled his wrists and ankles to the chair. My skirts whispered on the floor as I knelt beside him, drawing a thin dagger from my sleeve. His eyes widened, although whether it was because I was attempting to break him free just feet behind my Queen, or the dagger itself, I couldn't have said. I pressed a finger to my lips and inserted the dagger into the keyhole, then froze as I heard a sound behind me. I had been raised to that sound, and I stood slowly, holding the dagger out to the side and trying to push down the thrill of fear that rasp of steel shoved through me. Geneva held the sword almost lazily, but her body was tense, her eyes red and large. My tattoo flared so painfully that I hunched slightly, only years of training keeping me from crumpling into a ball of agony. Luka gripped my dress worriedly and rose out of the chair as far as he could, standing but pinned in place. The chains were barely long enough to allow him to stand, despite his worry over my well being; he would be no good in a fight.

"I see," Geneva said frigidly. "One of my Ladies has turned against her Queen. For a *man*." She sneered. "And a married one at that."

With each word she spoke, my alarm grew. This was not the Geneva I knew. She was almost mad, shifting constantly, her eyes too focused and unfocused in the same moment. I shifted forward, trying to push her away from Luka, who was defenseless if blades started swinging. It was a dangerous move, and we all knew it. By stepping close, I was putting myself easily in the range of her much longer sword, without giving myself an opening to strike with my short dagger. There was another hidden in my other sleeve, but I didn't dare draw it. Whatever madness had stolen over Geneva, I could only hope to draw her back to her senses before blood was shed.

"That's not true," I said carefully. Behind Gen, off the dais, I could see Loxxley being restrained by several guards. He was struggling to free himself, but we both knew he'd never get here in time. And that was fine. I could take care of this myself. "I brought him here, just as you asked. He came here in good faith, and yet, you put him in chains. If anyone has turned here, it is you."

"Because he is a danger to this kingdom, to my benevolent rule." Her eyes narrowed as she raised the sword, leveling it at my throat. She didn't seem so benevolent at the moment, but hopefully that would change if I could make her see sense. "And so are you."

I searched desperately for a way to get through to her. Something was so very wrong here, but I couldn't do anything to change her mind until we were alone. Here, there were far too many people. Only the War Ladies were armed, but judging by the looks on their faces, that would be enough of a problem by itself. I did the only thing I could.

"Queen Geneva. I challenge you to battle, with the prize being the throne. Win, and you may do what you wish to me. Lose, and you are mine to command."

Her face fell momentarily, but she shook her head and raised the sword. If she had thought that I was a threat to her throne, the path of least resistance would be to confirm her suspicions. "Fine. I accept your challenge." She motioned with her sword to the floor below the dais; the crowd shifted back, dresses swishing. I drew the dagger from my other sleeve and retreated down the stairs, meeting Loxxley's eyes as he was dragged back. With Geneva's longer sword, I was at an extreme disadvantage, but I didn't have a choice. Not for the first time, I wished that I had brought my sword, but there are only so many things that can be hidden in a fluffy dress, and a rapier is not one of them.

I raised my daggers, thick sleeves falling into the crooks of my elbows. I had bested Geneva before, and I could do it again. I had never wanted the throne, so I had never thought to challenge Geneva for it; she had thought her rule safe from me, of all people. And it would have been, if not for this sudden madness that had stolen over her like a smuggler in the dark of the harbor. We had been sparring partners for years, and I knew her strengths and weaknesses. She favored her right hand, so if I could force her to use the left, it would be to my advantage. I wanted to win the fight, but without killing her, which meant that I had to close the distance and stay inside her guard, without losing a limb or my life to the sword.

My train of strategy was derailed by Geneva taking a vicious swing at my head. I ducked beneath the blade and slashed with the dagger in my left hand, shredding the sleeve of her ice blue gown. A massive silver collar of mail extended over her collarbones and the tops of her breasts, glittering in the light and reminding me that she was better protected than I. The throbbing of my tattoo had subsided to a low throb, as it always did when I was fighting. It made sense that something enchanted to protect me from harm wouldn't actively attempt to get me killed. Thank heavens for small blessings, I suppose.

I may have bested Geneva in combat before, but I had been riding hard with Luka and Loxxley for days, not to mention my injuries. The cut on my left hand was almost entirely healed, but within a few minutes it was burning painfully from the tightness of my grip. My shoulder burned, not from the tattoo, but from the arrow wound. Geneva and I were both struggling to keep up the blistering pace that we had set, dancing back and forth, blades flashing, and trying not to listen to the gasps of the crowd. I had shredded both sleeves of her dress and opened several small wounds in her arms, as well as one larger one on her thigh. In return, she had delivered a slash to my face, one that hugged the curve of my cheekbone and bled sluggishly down my face. I needed a way to end this quickly, so I did the only thing I could think of: I tricked her. I slashed at her neck, intentionally leaving my side wide open. The sword flashed back and I lunged forward, well inside the range of the sword, dropping a dagger in order to grab her sword hand. A vicious twist and the blade clattered to the ground; she froze, my other dagger to her throat. Slowly, the crowd knelt. I backed away from Geneva, shoving down sadness as she levered herself slowly to her knees, wincing at the pain from her wounds. I hadn't wanted this, had never wanted this, but she hadn't left me much of a choice.

"Take her to the tower," I ordered the guards. "And release the War King." There were audible gasps from the crowd as they realized who Luka actually was; as soon as he was freed from his chains, he and Loxxley rushed to join me. Luka was staring at the slash on my face with a sort of horrified fascination; Loxxley, on the other hand, merely flipped my dagger in his palm and handed it to me after verifying that I was relatively unharmed.

Geneva climbed slowly to her feet, disdainfully waving away help from the guards. She raised her arms and the guards tensed, prepared for her to draw a weapon. Instead, she tossed her crown down, clattering at my feet, and drew herself up to her full height.

"I always knew you would betray me," she said. There was no emotion, which was chilling in itself. It was a statement of fact, as if my traitorous tendencies were as natural as the rising of the sun. It shook me to my core, but I tried to console myself with the thought that it was only her temporary madness speaking, although the thought smacked of untruthfulness. With her piece spoken, Geneva spun on her heel and stalked out of the room with the guards trailing behind her, every inch the Queen she had been. I wanted to sink to my knees and bawl, but that was unbecoming for a War Lady, let alone a Queen.

The partygoers dispersed. I spoke briefly with the guards, then saw everyone out the door, speaking only rarely. Throughout it all, Luka and Loxxley waited patiently on the other side of the doorway, just far enough back as to not be in the way, but still close enough to help if I needed it. Luka didn't seem irritated that no one was recognizing him as the War King, although a few people did nod or bow on their way out. None of my exiting guests commented on the slash on my cheek, which was dribbling sluggishly down to my chin. I doubted that this was the first duel for the throne that they had seen; they happened fairly often. Geneva had ruled for a few years now. Before her, the last War Queen had ruled for more than twenty years, through fear and viciousness. I had risen to my rank under her, but it was a long road for Geneva to regain her kingdom's trust. I could only hope that she hadn't done too much damage to that trust with her temporary madness.

Once everyone had left, the guards approached me, but most important was Zenin, the royal advisor. He bowed deeply and I nodded wearily. I wanted nothing to do with ruling a country, but until I figured out what had happened to Geneva, it looked like it was me who had things to do.

"What are you going to do with her?" Zenin asked. Typically the one who lost the fight for the crown was punished for the challenge, but I couldn't bring myself to say anything. My throat closed and I rubbed my wrists, one after the other. I couldn't do this right now. If ever I could.

"Later," I said roughly. "I need to rest." Zenin nodded and I hurried down the hallway, struggling to push down the tears. Too much had happened today, a friendship shattered, feelings that I wanted to hide brought to life, duties I had never wanted thrust upon me by necessity. The memories that Zenin's question had dredged up were the last thing I could take. I was nearly to my quarters when I heard running footsteps and turned, blinking away tears.

"What do you want?"

"What did she do to you?" Loxxley demanded. Luka was silent for once. He reached for my wrist, flipping it up before I could stop him. The sleeve of my dress slithered back to settle in the crook of my elbow, baring a vicious scar, raised and running horizontal across my wrist; part of it ran parallel to my other scars, straight lines that ran from side to side. My other wrist had an identical mark. Perhaps it was stress, or tiredness, or the fact that the two would be leaving soon and I would never see them again, but the words spilled from my lips, and I didn't try to stop them.

"The Queen before Geneva ruled as long as she did because she was vicious. Geneva challenged her once before she won, and lost. The Queen didn't take kindly to challengers, but she knew Geneva was a danger to her, so she took it out on the next best thing: me." I took a shaky breath. "She knew we were friends. Everyone did. When Geneva lost, she had her guards drag me to the top of the tower across from Geneva's. They tied my arms to the blade of my sword, and I couldn't free myself. I don't know how long I knelt there. It was meant as a lesson for Geneva, but I learnt something too. I never wanted to be Queen." The look of horror on their faces showed that they could understand how bad it had been. With my wrists tied to the blade, I couldn't move for fear of slitting myself open. The blade had rested across my shoulders, and there were scars there as well. To this day, I couldn't raise my arms above my head without pain. I wasn't ashamed of the scars, but I was ashamed of how I had acted. After days in the painful position, I had been so delirious I imagined my family being there, but I clearly remembered crying like a child. I vowed never to act that way again, and I hadn't, until now.

"I understand," Luka said softly.

"I doubt that," I said snappishly. "Loxxley, would you accompany me?" His brows rose, but he nodded slowly. I clicked my fingers and a guard approached from the end of the hall. "Please take- the War King to a guest chamber." I had to concentrate to remember to call him by his title rather than his name. I turned away and stepped into my chamber, or rather the outer solarium that joined the room where I slept, but not before I saw Luka's hurt expression. I refused to let myself care.

Loxxley followed me in, freezing when he saw the pair of eyes glittering in the dark corner. I had no such reservations, and neither did the dog. She leapt from her plush bed and into my arms; I grunted as she slammed into my chest, knocking me back a step. My dress pooled around me as I knelt, lowering her to the ground. Dare licked my throat eagerly, as she always did, but when her tongue started to swipe over the still bleeding slash on my face, I pulled her down by her thick leather collar. As much as I loved her, I didn't particularly want her saliva in an open wound. I rose and went to a chest in the corner of my room, which had all of my medical supplies.

When I turned back, Loxxley had taken my place on the floor, his long legs crossed. He was stroking Dare and dodging her enthusiastic tongue, his face split by a smile. It was the most unguarded I had seen him, and somehow, it made him look like Luka, made him approachable. I sat down next to him, laying the supplies out, and he jumped, immediately letting go of Dare and folding his hands in his lap. His head lowered, as if he were ashamed that he had been petting my dog. I shook my head, thinking once more how little I understood him.

"Don't stop on my account. Lord knows I can't give her all the affection that she needs. Loxxley, Dare. Dare, Loxxley." Dare lunged forward, licking him directly in the mouth as a greeting; he sputtered and I snickered. The grin returned, and again, it transformed his entire face.

"So why am I here? I assume it isn't to play with the dog, although if it is, I'm fine with that too." He stroked Dare's silky fur to prove his point.

"It's not. I was going to ask for your help taking care of this," I motioned to my cheek, which had finally stopped bleeding a few minutes before, when Dare had licked me, but had started up again when I grinned at Loxxley. "But if you want to keep playing with Dare, I can do it myself." I dipped a clean cloth into the deep bowl of water at my feet and started to scoot away to give them room, but a gentle hand on my thigh stopped me.

Loxxley took the cloth from me and shouldered Dare slightly away; she took the hint, and the commanding flick of the wrist from me, and returned to her bed. Her silky black ears dangled, shivering with the ecstatic wagging of her tail. She was lean and strong, with long black fur, the only thing about her that wasn't suited to hunting, the purpose that she had been bred for. She was the only one in her litter that had that soft fur. The breeder had offered her to me as a congratulations for my new status as a War Lady, and she had become one of the finest hunting hounds in the kingdom, second only to Geneva's hounds. We had learned many things together, but lately, I hadn't been able to give her the attention that she deserved because I had been away so much. Geneva wasn't the only friend that I had been neglecting.

My tattoo was dormant, slumbering peacefully. I couldn't

help but wonder why it had alerted me to Loxxley in the beginning but didn't now. Who knew? The ways of an enchanted tattoo were hardly up to me to explain. The cloth was red with dried blood. Loxxley swiped it gently over the wound, his other hand cupped around my chin to hold me in place. I couldn't help but think how this must look, of how close we were sitting, the thick velvet of my dress splayed across both of our legs, part of my legs bare, his hand on my face. I didn't move. Once the wound was clean, he smeared a salve on it, then washed his hands in the bowl of water and stood. I took his offered hand and rose also.

"I know I wasn't your first choice, but I'm glad I could help," he said quietly. I couldn't help but smile, grim as it was.

"Actually, you were my first choice. You're the only one who wouldn't simper about how it would ruin my pretty face, or how much it must hurt, or how I did the right thing. Sometimes it's nice to be treated as an equal, not as a competitor or a noble. It's nice," I repeated. He was stroking Dare, who had her head pressed against his thigh as she gazed adoringly at him. His gaze was wistful.

"I've always wanted a dog," he admitted. "Luka has Rupert. All of the others have a dog, but I've never been able to find the right one. Plus, I'm a bit scared of them." He rolled up his sleeve, where a set of faded teeth marks shone on his skin. Canine teeth marks. "I've mostly gotten over it. Mostly." I nodded understandingly, thanking him again and seeing him out the door without having my attention fully on him, my mind whirling. I had an idea, but it would have to wait until the morning. Tonight, I had a mystery to solve.

Chapter Sixteen

I exited my chambers, close on the heels of the man in front of me. We grinned at one another as he kissed my cheek gently and headed down the hallway, but my smile dropped as Luka met my eyes. Or rather, he glared. Loxxley was completely impassive, as he often was. He nodded at the man's retreating back.

"I didn't realize that you would spend a night like last night with someone."

"I would imagine that there are quite a few things you don't know about me. We don't really know one another at all," I said frigidly. His eyes flashed with hurt, but I didn't react. In fact, it was not what they thought at all, but I was required by no one to explain myself, even before I was the Queen. I had already been up for several hours this morning, and run the errands that I needed to. Now I was on to confront the cause of Geneva's illness, and I didn't have time to deal with Luka's jealousy. "If you'll excuse me." I stepped past him and strode down the hallway with my head held high.

Lana glanced up from the papers on the desk. Geneva's desk, or mine now, I supposed. She smiled slightly, but I didn't return it. I didn't have time for the niceties.

"I didn't know that you wanted to be Queen."

The smile dropped from her lips. "I don't know what you're referring to."

"I think you do. I think you paid one of the kitchen girls very well to slip a drug into every one of Geneva's meals, one that would make her paranoid, weaken her. As best as I can tell, this has been going on for months. So just don't."

Lana was never one to stick with a dying cause. Now that she knew I knew, she didn't bother to stay with her pretense. She drew her daggers, holding them easily, and I felt only the briefest twinge of warning from my tattoo. There was more of a twinge of irony, since I had given those daggers to her as a midwinter gift a few years ago; now she was going to try and kill me with them. Emphasis on the *try*, I hoped.

"That didn't take as long as I expected," she mused. "I thought that it would be at least a few days in your new position before you found that girl. She never was very trustworthy, anyway. Obviously."

"Maybe you aren't as smart as you think." Her face tightened, as did the grip on her daggers as I drew my own sword with a rasp of steel. I was back in my favorite outfit, weapons and all, with one addition: a crown. Geneva's maidservant, who was polite to me but was not nearly so friendly or attentive as my own servants, had brought out several crowns and refused to let me leave until I had chosen one. In frustration, I had chosen the simplest one, dark iron studded with tiny star shaped sapphires. It still didn't feel quite right, but I was doing my best to ignore it. I wore a deep blue dress that sparkled, not from some sort of stones, but from chain mail woven into it. Beneath it I wore black trousers, with greaves layered over to protect my shins. The high collar was also layered with mail, front and back, with more to protect my back and insides. Short boots with metallic inserts in the toes melded seamlessly with the greaves, leaving gap for a blade to pierce.

"How did you figure it out? It was rather fast, even for the magical warrior," she mocked, flicking her dagger toward my tattoo; I flinched before I could stop myself. She wasn't going to throw it at me, but it was an instinctive reaction. The only reason I was sure that she wouldn't throw it was that she was accustomed to using twin daggers and good as she was, she might not be able to adapt to only having one.

"She admitted it, when I went to the kitchen this morning and caught her putting a few drops of clear liquid onto a plate of food. It was for me, but it didn't take much time to convince her to tell me the truth about Geneva's "illness." She had been drugging Geneva for months, and she told me she had standing orders to continue with the next Queen. "Should I be flattered that you thought of me as enough of a threat to drug me, or just offended?"

"Perhaps both. Although, it's not personal. My plan was to continue drugging each Queen to paranoia, then swoop in, take the throne, and regain the people's trust."

"You'd be the savior. They'd do anything for you, and no one would ever suspect foul play." I chuckled darkly. "Lord knows this life is enough to drive us over the edge."

She nodded, not surprised that I had figured it out. "However, since you know, the plan has changed. You understand. With your King here, and the spat outside your chambers this morning, it won't be difficult to convince people that you had a lover's quarrel. Two fighters, and your notoriously volatile temper, his a virtual unknown. It's no surprise that you both end up dead."

She slashed easily at me, far too slowly to have been an actual attack. I skipped backward and my tattoo flared viciously; I doubled over with a short gasp of pain, the blade of a sword whistling over my exposed back. I spun sideways to return, parrying the sword away, but the situation was grim. Lana was in no hurry to kill me. I had ordered this end of the castle to be left alone this morning, at least until I figured out what to do next, so even if I shouted, there was no one to hear. Lana's cronies crowded in behind her, brandishing their weapons. She hung back and watched as I traded blows with her cronies, putting my back to the wall so that none of the men could sneak up behind me. I slashed viciously, opening enough space to draw a throwing knife, but before I could throw it, a voice yelled out.

"Stop!" Everyone froze, including me. The tip of Luka's sword rested between Lana's shoulder blades; Loxxley stood beside his brother, his own blade keeping the rest of the thugs at bay; he twitched it in warning when one of the thugs moved and he shrank away. I shoved my way free of the crush and sheathed my sword, nodding gratefully at the boys. Several of the palace guard panted into the room. Although they were several minutes late, I didn't want to be the one to take another of my friends to the dungeon; I couldn't help but feel that two in two days was a bad omen. However, I could rectify that, since only one of them actually deserved to be punished.

Loxxley must have sensed my fuming resistance to speaking with Luka, because he placed himself between us as we crossed the courtyard and ascended a set of stairs behind a thick wooden door, guarded by two burly guards that dipped their heads respectfully at me. There were too many stairs to count; my calves burned, but it wasn't any worse than I'd had before. The stairs were narrower and narrower as we reached the top, so narrow that Loxxley had to drop back, with Luka behind him. Small guttering torches hung in iron braziers at regular intervals, with more distance between the ones at the top as natural light seeped in through cracks in the stone. Dust collected on each step, disturbed only recently by the guards and the tower's newest inhabitant. This particular tower had been abandoned for years. There was a rumor that it was haunted, and I would not have been surprised if that were true, but for Geneva and me, there were more earthly reasons to avoid it like the plague that had taken the lives of my parents. Painful memories that made the agony from my tattoo feel like the pinprick of a needle.

The door at the top wasn't guarded, but I had the key, so I didn't need anyone to open it for me. I pulled the key, hanging from its thin golden chain, from beneath the neck of my dress; neither of my companions could see what I was doing, but they didn't question it. The door's old hinges creaked as it opened and I tensed, ready for a confrontation, but Geneva was in plain view. She was sitting on the narrow bed in the room, staring out the window, shoulders hunched. Her long hair, escaping from its careful updo, dangled around her face, hiding her from view.

"Gen?" I said softly.

Geneva's head shot up, and she lurched unsteadily to her feet. She was still wearing what she had had on the night before, now rumpled and bloody from our short fight. The soft ivory of the bandages beneath flashed each time she moved. A fresh dress hung on a hook on the wall, although why she hadn't put it on, I couldn't have said. She rushed forward and embraced me, burying her face in my shoulder, or as well as she could with the difference in our heights. I flexed my knees so that she wasn't leaning on my hard collarbone.

"I'm sorry. I haven't felt like myself in a long time, but I could never have imagined that I would do something like that." She pulled back and looked at Luka. She hesitated, then bent her knee in a half-hearted curtsey. Only when I noticed Luka's puzzled expression did I realize why she had paused. As Queen, she and Luka would have addressed one another as equals, and since this was her kingdom, technically he would bow to her. However, she wasn't Queen anymore. I was. No doubt she was still recovering from her sudden drop in status and was unsure how to behave. "My apologies to you as well, my Lord." This time, the curtsey was much deeper and more prolonged. Luka nodded in acknowledgement, and she rose stiffly.

I motioned at Loxxley, who was standing so close behind me that his broad chest brushed the back of my shoulder with each breath. "Geneva, this is Loxxley. Loxxley, Geneva." They greeted one another politely, and Geneva seemed more comfortable, perhaps because they were roughly equal in status, or at least that was what she hoped; I could see it in her eyes. When a War Queen lost the battle for her crown, the new Queen could choose whether she would be knocked down to second in command or if she would start over from the bottom, above only the newest of recruits. I hadn't given it much thought prior to this moment, but as far as I was concerned, the moment she was fit to return to duty, this crown would be back on her head. If I hadn't been afraid that she'd have us all beheaded the moment the crown was back on her head, I would have tossed it at her and been the first to clap at her coronation.

I asked the boys to give us a moment and they excused themselves politely. Geneva and I had a lot to talk about, not least of which was what we would do about the crown currently resting on my head. They nodded and retreated down the stairs, closing the door quietly behind them. Luka glanced back once, as if unsure whether or not it was safe to leave me alone with her, but Loxxley was already gone; his hand appeared around the door and he hauled his brother away by the front of his shirt. I seated myself on the short stool in the corner, giving

Geneva the choice of where to sit. She chose to sit on the bed, back against the wall, arms wrapped around her knees.

"I'm sorry," I said softly. "I know how hard it must be for you to be in this tower. I fought with myself about it before the order, but I couldn't bear to send you to the dungeons. Perhaps it would have been easier for you that way."

She shook her head. "I needed to face my fears sometime. This way isn't easy for me, but I don't imagine that it's any easier for you." As if answering some unknown call, both of our heads swiveled toward the window. Across the way, at the same level, the flat roof of another tower was easily visible. There was where I had knelt as punishment for Geneva's challenge, and this tower was where she had watched me suffer. I could feel the ghostly shivers of pain roll through my tattoo, but I wasn't going to dwell on it.

"How is your shoulder?" It struck me as ironic that both of our shoulders had been injured recently, although mine was mostly healed. She shrugged and made a dismissive motion with her hand. I could see that it had already been cared for, so I didn't push the issue. We continued to speak about more important things, for hours.

The sky was darkening to ebony by the time I left Geneva's tower. Luka and Loxxley were leaving in the morning, with the peace talks on hold until the decision was made as to who the Queen would be going forward. As the acting War Queen, it was my job to see them off. I had gotten to the bottom of the conspiracy against Geneva, and almost everything had been explained. Lana had admitted that she had orchestrated all of the ambushes against us, including the one in which my tattoo had been injured. Geneva had already seemed much better, and I hoped that she would be back to ruling form very soon. The only real problem was Luka, and how I may or may not have felt about him. I couldn't shake the feeling that there could have been more between us, but I did my best to forget about it. He was King, and I never wanted to be Queen. I had lived my life happily without a man for this long; it made no real sense that my world would be upended the moment the boy with the crooked crown stepped into it, but there it was. I could only hope that things would change, and they did.

Chapter Seventeen

I tightened Sin's girth, pushing down the urge to draw a blade when I felt someone's presence at my back. I turned and sidled sideways, trying not to seem suspicious. Luka seemed too preoccupied to notice, his eyes dark and pained, but Loxxley's clever eyes followed my every move. The subterfuge would only be necessary for a few minutes longer, so I urged the boys onto their mounts. They obliged, and I pushed Sin into a canter almost before they were in their saddles. Although, technically, I only had to see them off, I was escorting them to a field on the outskirts of the city, where their retinue waited. There was a reason that I was in such a hurry, and it was about to be revealed.

Soon, drab gray stone turned to green grass beneath the horses' hooves. I pulled Sin to a stop and swung off, not bothering to speak to the entourage. I felt bad for ignoring them, but they would have to wait.

Luka looked startled and puzzled, but Loxxley just leaned forward on his saddle, his lips quirked up.

"Out with it. Whatever's got you so happy."

"Can't I just be happy?" He quirked an eyebrow and I grinned, fumbling with the straps of my saddlebag. Finally I calmed down enough to loosen the buckles and reach inside. The black puppy was quiet, but that didn't mean that she wasn't excited. I had already taught her the command for quiet, and the brilliant, keen creature that she was, she had not made a peep the entire ride. Cuddling her to my chest, I stopped next to Loxxley's horse and offered him the puppy, almost shyly. His eyes widened, and he slowly reached for her, as if he were afraid of hurting her. She had no such qualms. Her claws scraped my arms as she leapt into his lap; his white stallion twitched but didn't move. Loxxley lifted the puppy carefully and pressed her to his chest, his long fingers stroking her thick black fur, so unlike her mother's.

"Is this…?" Loxxley began. Luka still looked puzzled, but then, he hadn't seen Dare last night. For that, I was glad. One part of my life, at least, that wouldn't be tainted by the memories of the crooked crown King. I could remember Loxxley's face, the happiness in his eyes, and I was glad I had shared her with him.

I nodded. "One of Dare's pups. They are ready to go to their new homes, and I can't think of a better home than with you." I flushed. I hadn't meant to say so much, but it was too late now.

He swung his leg over the saddle and slid down to speak with me; I was glad, because my neck was beginning to hurt from staring up at him on his tall stallion. To my shock, he hugged me, wrapping his free arm around my shoulders and holding the puppy tightly with the other. I hugged him back. His grin was wider than I had ever seen it, and I couldn't help but notice how close we were standing, with only the puppy between us. She chose that moment to make herself known, lunging upward to lick our faces; she managed to get my chin and Loxxley's lips. He sputtered and I burst out laughing, dodging her flicking tongue.

Luka spoke, his voice soft. "Tara. May I speak with you?" A refusal was on my lips, but I made the mistake of looking at him. His shoulders were hunched as he faced toward me, his face pained. He seemed so badly to want to speak to me, that I couldn't tell him no. If nothing else, I respected him enough to explain why I never wanted to see him again. It would be easier for both of us that way. He would forget about me in a month or two, or as soon as he was married, and would only remember the warrior who had helped to defend him. For that was all I was, and that was all I ever would be to him.

I came to stand by his horse and he dismounted. Geneva had given him a horse more befitting a War King, so rather than the old gelding who had so patiently carried him, he now had another white stallion, one of the few stallions in the royal stables. I couldn't help but wonder what had happened to his other horse, but right now I was glad of this one, whose bulk hid us from the rest of the party. I lowered my head, twisting the fingers of my left hand in the stallion's long white mane.

"Yes, Luka." I swallowed hard, already regretting my word choice. It would be easier for both of us if we weren't so familiar. I had to remember that. "Your Majesty."

His face fell. My heart twisted at the pain I had caused, but it couldn't be helped. "I'm sorry. Sorry for everything. That I didn't tell you about my upcoming marriage before now."

So was I. If I had known, it might have prevented heartbreak for both of us. Then again, it might not have. "And I'm sorry that I didn't realize my Queen was going insane and wanted to kill you."

Luka's full lips cracked a smile. "To be fair, she tried to kill you first." I nodded.

"I'm glad that I could meet you. This was an adventure, to say the least, but we won't have another one together." He frowned in confusion, but I plunged on. "We will never see each other again. That is my wish."

"As you wish," he said sadly. His lips brushed my cheek with the gentlest of touches before he climbed onto his horse, never once meeting my eyes. "Brother. Bring your new pet and come away. We need to be going."

Loxxley frowned, tilting his head down, his long blond hair falling into his eyes. I wanted to brush it back, but before I could, he kissed my cheek gently and climbed back onto his horse, cuddling the puppy to his chest. Luka kicked his horse into motion, and Loxxley moved to follow, but before he could, I grabbed his boot. Even through the leather, I could feel the muscle tense in surprise.

"Write to me." It sounded like a command, but really it was a quiet plea. Perhaps it would be nice to have a friend that I wouldn't have to throw in the dungeon. If I even could. "I'd like to know what you name the pup. I hope that she'll serve you as faithfully as her mother has for me."

"I'm sure she will."

The white stallion spun and cantered away. I watched them go, my hand resting on Sin's thick neck. I was sad to see them go, especially Loxxley. I had mixed feelings about Luka, but I still didn't want to see him go. He was taken, and there could never have been a future for us, but that didn't change the fact that I cared about him. I thought I might be in love, but the more I thought about it, I didn't know what love was. I never had, but maybe someday I could learn. Just not with Luka.

Reluctantly, I returned to the castle. Geneva had been released the night before, and already she was much improved. We had agreed that I would be the War Queen for now, and once she was back to full strength, I would abdicate and return the throne to her, she who actually wanted it. I was looking forward to that day, but until it came, I had work to do. Perhaps then, I could begin to feel what I needed to, and to heal. Once that was finished, I would hunt down Eili's killer and gain justice for her slaying. I owed it to her.

Epilogue

I sighed deeply, flopping back onto the chaise lounge in my quarters. The massive windows were dark, lit only by the stars outside and the tall lamps scattered throughout the city. It was deep into the night, and I would rather have been at my own home, but I couldn't bring myself to ride home. I just wanted to sleep, but as much as I wanted to, sleeping on a chaise in a velvet dress and with tightly coiled hair would likely not be very comfortable. I heaved myself off the chaise and headed into the next room, beginning the long process of pulling the countless pins from my long curls. They clinked onto the dressing table one by one, releasing my long brown hair from its bonds.

It had been more than a month since I had seen Loxxley and Luka. Every week since, a rider had arrived from Mareen, bearing a letter from Loxxley, updating me on the progress now that the mole in his castle had finally been discovered, thanks to information that Lana had revealed. He also made sure to keep a running commentary on the growth of his new companion, whom he had chosen to name Liberty. I smiled each time I read about her, not just because I was relieved that Dare's pup was doing well, but also from the joy that infused every word Loxxley wrote about her in his neat, tiny handwriting. I could hear his words in my ear with every stroke of the pen. I kept all of his letters carefully locked away in a trunk in my room, my own private secret that everyone knew about. They were the talk of the castle, but I didn't care. As far as anyone knew, I had been sent to bring the War King here in disguise, which was the truth. When they questioned why it had been me that had been sent rather than one of the others, Geneva's excuse had been that I had been saddened by my possible link to Eili's death and she had sent me because the ride would do me good. The looks of pity increased along with the whispers, but for now, the secret of my magical tattoo was safe.

Luka had tried to write as well, but after the first few had been returned to him unopened, with only a short missive that I had sent congratulating him on his announced engagement, he had stopped trying. According to Loxxley, he was hurting, but I refused to let myself care, and instead threw myself into helping Geneva return to her status as beloved Queen.

Geneva glanced up, her slender hand pausing in her writing of a letter. She seemed different now that she wasn't trying to hide her vulnerability. No longer did she snap to attention when someone entered a room, saving her energy and her strength for when she needed it most. Now that I wasn't afraid she was going to have someone beheaded in a bad mood, I could sleep in my own home at night. My only missions lately had been slow and uneventful; I had mostly been around the city, keeping the peace and breaking up the occasional drunken brawl.

"Tara. I wasn't expecting you yet."

I frowned, stroking Dare's floppy ears gently. Geneva's hounds were sprawled out on the rug by the fireplace, their woven collars a splash of color against the flickering of the flames. It was so early in the morning that I wouldn't have thought that she would be awake, but I should have known better; she seemed never to sleep. She was working hard to regain her former status, and I was working hard to help her. I had spent most of the day mingling around town, visiting a few innkeepers to check that their taxes would be paid on time.

I had gone home to eat and brought Dare out with me; with all of her puppies in good homes and with me stuck in the city until further notice, she had been climbing the walls. My servants had registered a subtle complaint at our clear unhappiness, and I had decided to take pity on them. Laith had found me on my way home and told me that Geneva wanted to see me; rather than running home and then coming back, I had just come to the castle. Now I had to find out what she wanted.

"Sit, please." I did, still stroking Dare. Geneva sank into her chair as well, folding her soft blue dress out of the way. A round sapphire graced her slender neck, an iron tiara with matching stones perched on her thick hair.

"Why did you need to see me?"

Geneva pushed a page across her desk, which was otherwise mostly empty. She hadn't left the castle much since the disastrous ball, having said that she couldn't muster the bravery to face her people just yet. She would have to soon, to go on progress with us. After Eili's death, progress had been disrupted, but we would still have to go soon in order to see to the state of affairs. It was only a matter of time.

I lifted the page curiously, and my heart plummeted. Dare whined; I loosened my fingers where they were tangled in her thick fur. The handwriting was familiar. I hadn't seen it like this before, since I hadn't actually opened any of his letters, but I did recognize the looping, crooked script. This was Luka's handwriting.

To Geneva, War Queen of Antille,

I know that our one meeting was less than fortuitous, and that you offered me any assistance that you could provide, in order to repair the relationship between our two countries. I write you now to beg for your help. My betrothed was on her way to my kingdom for our wedding when she was taken hostage. My own warriors can find no indication of her, but I know who could. I ask that you send Tara to our aid, so that she may assist us in finding my beloved. I would consider it a personal favor if you would send her. She has not responded to any of my letters, but I know that she will listen to you, and that you will not let our past encounters close your ears to my pleas.

In hope,
Luka, War King of Mareen

I dropped the letter like it had burned me, scuffing my fingers on my dress as if I could wash it away. I couldn't help but feel a perverse sense of satisfaction that something had happened to his other woman, which I immediately felt guilty for. This girl couldn't help who she was betrothed to. I couldn't even be angry with Luka. He had done what he had to do to save his people, like any leader would; it had been noble. He couldn't back out of the agreement. His previous engagement wasn't going to change just because I had felt the first stirrings of feelings in a long time. Life went on, but that didn't mean that I wanted to be the one to find his lover. I wished her no harm, but I wished to never see either of them again.

I met Geneva's eyes, not bothering to hide my feelings. I could tell that she was conflicted, and I braced myself for the bad news. Dare whined again.

"You have to understand," she said helplessly. She was winding a ring around her finger. It was silver and quite bulky, held onto her biggest finger only because of the string wound around the inside. An inscription was barely visible, disappearing beneath the string: *With love, E.*

Despite my own troubles in love, I couldn't help but smirk, for I recognized that ring. That was Ellis's ring, which explained why the yarn was necessary to help it fit. The inscription was new. That must have been one of the reasons why she seemed so reluctant to send me, but she had a duty to her people. Sending me on this mission at the personal request of a nearby monarch would provide serious leverage if she ever needed it in the future. Luka had known that when he wrote the letter, and times must be dire in need that he would hand out a favor like that.

"Please don't make me," I said softly, although I knew I wouldn't change her mind. How could I, in the face of every-thing that had happened? She needed support now more than ever; it was the only way that she could rebuild her reputation and the trust of her kingdom.

"I don't have a choice. I need this. The kingdom needs this. Please, do this for me."

I glared at her. "I am not the War Queen," I said frigidly. "I am tired of doing everything for the good of the kingdom. Just once, I will do something for myself. Find someone else to do this, or I will be forced to resign my commission." I shot to my feet. Geneva's eyes were cold, and she stood as well, making fierce eye contact.

"I didn't want to have to do this. Think of Luka. You would see the man you love suffer, when there is something that you can do to alleviate his pain?" I opened my mouth to protest, but she threw something onto the table. A bundle of creamy paper, each with a broken seal. I picked one up. The thick paper was covered with familiar handwriting: Luka's. When I had sent these letters back to him, the seals had been intact, since I hadn't even opened them. It looked like they had never made it back to him. "I know you love him. If you didn't, you would have responded to his letters. The fact that you didn't is a mark of how much you care about him."

"What have you done?"

She chuckled darkly and took the letter back. "I've already sent the response back. Do this for me, and you will be be outside of my orders from now on. You will have your rank and your title, but you will no longer be under my command."

"No." She raised her brows, waiting expectantly for my response. "I will do this, for Luka and Loxxley. After that, we are finished."

I stalked out, Dare on my heels. Apparently Geneva had not been as recovered as I thought, but it was no longer my concern. I had thought once that she was my friend, but that was no longer the case. I would find Luka's betrothed, for him and for her, and then I would retire. A quiet life would perhaps be welcome, and it would give me the chance to recover from my sickness in love. Perhaps I would find happiness once more, but only after I had tracked down Eili's killers. That would be my last act as a warrior.

Sin reared, driving Geneva back. She watched warily; I glared at her and didn't even try to bring my huge mount to a standstill. As far as I was concerned, being this close to Geneva was still far too close. The fact that she had stooped to blackmailing me meant that she was not as healed as I had hoped, but it was no longer my concern.

"Are you certain that this is what you want?" Geneva asked. She watched Sin warily. Sin was sidling sideways on the hard cobbles, ears pinned flat, despite my tight grip on the reins.

"I'm certain," I said shortly. "The next time you see me, it will be for me to turn in my commission. This is what you've done to me."

About the Author

Julie Kramer hails from a small town in Ohio, USA. Her debut novel is already receiving high praise on Amazon including "A thrilling read" and "Well developed storyline - the writing is flawless".

Julie Kramer recently graduated from college and has a black belt in Taekwondo. When not writing about dragons, griffins, and other fantasy creatures, she works at a restaurant and looks after her two beloved dogs - a Husky and a Yorkie.

Made in the USA
Columbia, SC
25 March 2023

14284119R00090